John Wesley Ha

John Harvey is a prolific writer of westerns and thrillers; he also writes children's fiction and poetry, and edits and publishes a magazine of writing and photography called *Slow Dancer*. At present he is doing research and a little teaching in the American Studies department of Nottingham University. He likes watching movies and one or two other things.

In the same series:

Hart One: Cherokee Outlet
Hart Two: Blood Trail
Hart Three: Tago
Hart Four: The Silver Lie
Hart Five: Blood on the Border
Hart Six: Ride the Wide Country
Hart Seven: Arkansas Breakout

John B. Harvey

Hart Eight:
John Wesley Hardin

Pan Original
Pan Books London and Sydney

First published 1982 by Pan Books Ltd,
Cavaye Place, London SW10 9PG

ISBN 0 330 26641 1
Photoset by Parker Typesetting Service, Leicester
Printed in Great Britain by
Collins, Glasgow

For Cathy:
for keeping cool when it was needed most

One

High summer 1865

The sound of the riders preceded them like thunder low on the wind. There were twelve of them, white and black, spurring their horses across the swirl of Texas plain. Light filtered off the rim of eastern horizon, illuminating the motes of dust which flew like sparks above their heads.

They rode in a rough column of threes, their ragged military formation accentuated by the fact that several of the riders wore remnants of army uniform. A pair of patched blue pants with a yellow stripe down the outside of the legs; a private's service dress jacket with only one yellow epaulette remaining, and that hanging by mere threads and flapping wildly; the green-collared and -cuffed jacket of the Irish Brigade, presently worn by a fierce-looking black with a shaven head and thick beard; three faded kepis, one of which had lost part of its peak – none of these compared to the dress of the man at the front and centre of the column.

Tall and broad, he wore a black felt Hardee hat with the crown punched up so that it sloped to a point. The brim rose up steeply at one side and was held in place by a shield and eagle brass badge, the rest sagging downwards. A stunted black plume was attached to one side of the hatband, fastened inside a yellow hatcord. At the front, the crossed sabres and insignia sloped steeply to the right.

The face beneath the hat was florid and moustached, a diagonal scar running from in front of the left ear almost to the edge of the full-lipped mouth. The man's stomach swelled out against a darned and sweat-stained red vest, over which he was wearing a dark green frock coat that had once belonged to a sergeant in G company of the First Regiment of Sharpshooters.

A civilian-issue gun belt was buckled tight round a pair of light blue pants, pushed down into high leather boots. Two holsters were attached to the belt, each containing a .36 calibre Colt Navy revolver.

A smile drifted over his face like a cloud as he saw in the middle distance the blurred outlines of the farmhouse taking shape through the shimmer of heat haze ahead.

The rider alongside, a stubble-chinned man in buckskin pants and jacket, hauled his mount close and called, 'That her, R.G.?'

R.G. Archibald nodded his head and tasted the back-bite of bile at the roof of his mouth. Sure, that was the home of that Reb bastard who'd called him a coward and a nigger-lover and reckoned he was going to get away with it on account of him being six-handed at the time and R.G. on his own. That was where the bastard lived. R.G. looked quickly over his shoulder at the line of riders. Only this time strength was all on his side.

'Yeah,' he yelled back, his voice barely audible above the driving sound of the horses, 'that's her right enough.'

Vinnie was squatting in the yard, back of the family wagon, engaged in what was almost his favourite occupation. After going hunting with his pa at first light, the two dogs running on ahead of them like ghosts through the misted grass; after watching his ma in the kitchen when she made cakes, biting down softly into her bottom lip the way she did when she was concentrating, him knowing that when she was done he'd be allowed to wipe the end of his finger round the inside of the mixing bowl; after skinny-dipping in the creek along with his sister – except that now she was growing apace, she always scolded him not to look until she was covered by the water. If he'd been asked, Vinnie would likely have said those were the things he liked doing best. And after them came keeping silent and still as he could, watching the cat stalk birds.

The cat was a small tabby his father had brought back from town when it was still small enough to sleep in his shoe. Several months old now and sleek, it was growing into a handsome animal, with white forepaws and a white smudge close to the end of its tail. In the daytime, it would sleep in the shade of the barn, rush in front of anyone who set foot outside the house and roll on to its back in order that its belly could be stroked, try to climb into the milking bucket, chase anything from straw and its own tail to Vinnie's shadow – and do its stealthy best to catch birds.

Which was what it was doing now.

Pad, pad, pause, pad – body elongated and the button nose stretched out towards the young blackbird less than a dozen yards away.

Vinnie held his breath.

Pad, pause, pad.

A quick, silent scurry and the bird's head ducked up, yellow beak shining, but its wings stayed down.

Vinnie tried to ignore the tightening pain in the muscles at the backs of his legs.

Pad, pad, pad.

Quicker than the boy's eyes could clearly follow, the cat launched itself forward. There was a swirl of feathers, a piping call of alarm, a scattering cloud of dust. For a few moments it looked as though the bird might struggle free from the cat's mouth, one black wing flapped and fanned and the cat shook its prey like a dog. Vinnie moved into a crouch, rubbing away the cramp from the back of his thigh.

The bird still shrilly piping, the cat began to trot with it towards the front door of the house.

'Ma! The cat's got . . .'

But Vinnie's mother no longer needed telling. She was in the doorway, aproned and armed with a rolling pin.

'Damn you for a cruel specimen!'

'Aw, Ma!'

His mother ignored his protest and advanced slowly on the cat, showing him enough of the rolling pin to make the animal back off, its belly trailing the dust, the wing flapping less and less energetically in its face.

'What in the Lord's name—?'

Vinnie took a few moments to realize that his mother was no longer talking about the cat; she wasn't even looking at it any more, but there, back past the picket fence, out on to the plain.

'Vinnie!'

The boy froze at the pitch of her voice.

'Vinnie, run off an' fetch your pa!'

He stared at her, unmoving.

'Go on now. Do like I say!'

Vinnie stuttered into motion, his bare feet skidding on the dirt, arms flailing wide as he skittered across the yard. Startled, the cat jumped aside and the blackbird flew out of his mouth, straight into the branches of the skimpy tree past the barn end. Amazed and open-mouthed, the cat stared after it. Vinnie's feet took him around the side of the house, clambering over the corral fence, between three horses penned inside, over the fence at the far side and past the pile of drying dung towards where his father had been working at the vegetable patch.

The man looked up as he heard his son running, straightened his back with a groan and arched it across the fingers of his right hand. He wiped the sweat from his eyes with his bare arm, smearing himself with dirt.

'Pa!'

Vinnie's father lifted the fork one-handed and stuck it half-tine deep in the hard earth. He could see the dust now, hear the rumble of hoofs low to the ground; he no longer needed the boy's breathless words of warning. With haste he moved towards his son, clasping the back of his head with a caring firmness and turning him, hurrying him to the back door of the house.

Inside, he saw to his satisfaction that his wife had already bolted and barred the front door and that she was ordering their daughter, March, to close and bolt the window shutters while she saw to loading the two rifles – a long-barrelled Sharps and a muzzle-loading Springfield musket – and readying the

Dance Brothers copy of a .44 Colt Army that her husband had carried through the War Between the States.

For a second the eyes of husband and wife met across the low-ceilinged room, met, locked and passed on.

'Pa!'

The man nudged his son aside, hurrying to fasten the back door. He collided with him again on his way towards the table and by this time the boy was crying, his arms by his sides, air being gulped nervously into his mouth as he stood stupidly frightened and not understanding why.

His father pulled out the wooden peg behind one of half a dozen movable slats just wide enough to allow a rifle barrel to push through and permit an eye to sight along the top. His mother went to the opposite side of the front door and did the same. Vinnie hesitated, began to run towards his elder sister, finally bit down on his lower lip, wiped at his face with his shirt tail and said as boldly as he could, 'Who is it, Pa?'

His father didn't move his head, didn't answer.

'Pa?'

'Vinnie!' called his mother angrily. 'Hush up!'

The boy turned on his heels, smarting, trying to keep back the tears that were again prickling at the backs of his eyes. March went quietly to him and put an arm round his shoulder but he shrugged her off and stood defiantly away.

The man had recognized the leader of the riders by now; he had him in the sights of the Sharps, the red vest between the flapping sides of his green uniform coat. His finger grazed the trigger. One shot would, should, drop him from the saddle dead. If they were lucky they might deal with three more before the remainder, enraged, tore the place apart.

Without turning his head, he thought about his children. He thought about the scum outside, Northern trash riding with niggers, despoiling all of Texas if they could.

Reconstruction!

The word caught inside his brain like a burr.

He'd reconstruct the sons of bitches . . .

'Henry,' said his wife, her voice unnaturally husky, 'I don't reckon they want anything more than to cuss and fire off a few shots. Maybe run off the horses.'

'You sayin' we should let 'em?'

The woman glanced at her children and the man knew what she was thinking, his finger continued to hesitate on the trigger and the back of his throat went dry as drought.

'Get out of there, you Rebel bastard!'

'Stop hidin' behind your woman's skirts!'

'Face us like a man, why don't you?'

'Hell, that's easy. What we got here ain't no man, it's just Southern trash wearin' pants as don't fit.'

Guffaws of laughter swept from man to man. The black in the Irish Brigade jacket pulled a bottle of whisky from one of his saddle bags, jerked the cork with his teeth and swallowed mouthful upon mouthful until he was gasping for breath and the liquor was running down both sides of his mouth and into the dark wire-wool of his beard.

'Pass it here!' called R.G. and caught the bottle with a swaggering laugh when the Negro hurled it through the air.

The plumed hat dipped back as the bottle was raised, swept down again as R.G. shouted and tossed the whisky to another hand. So it went until the last drop had been drained and then a Mexican half-breed in a kepi lifted the empty bottle high above his head and hurled it against the thick wood of the door.

At the sound of smashing glass Vinnie cried out and turned towards his sister, who grabbed him close and shushed him against her chest.

'Get out here, yeller-belly!' called R.G. and a shout of impatience went up from the men with him, some of their mounts turning about and then about again.

'I could make a hole in his head big enough to run my hand clear through,' the father said ruefully, speaking more to himself than anybody else.

As if in answer several of the men outside pulled their pistols and fired them in the direction of the house. Shots ricocheted away from the timber harmlessly, accompanied by a holler of approval.

R. G. Archibald flicked the reins of the big chestnut and came a further ten yards forward so that he was at the entrance to the yard. He leaned back in the saddle and pointed his gloved hand towards the house.

'Ain't so full of sass an' vinegar now, Mister Johnny Reb, are you? Ain't so quick to go shootin' off at the mouth when you ain't got a dozen men backin' you up. No! You're sneakin' around in there, pokin' that rifle of yours through peep-holes and makin' damn sure you don't risk hide nor hair gettin' hurt.'

The gloved index finger pointed towards the barrel end of the Sharps. 'Hidin' back of your woman's skirts like the coward you are. Stinkin' yeller like a cringin' dog an' you ain't got the balls to come out and face me like a man. If I were you I'd be so shamed right now I wouldn't have the guts to look any son of mine in the face.'

Several of the men back of him yelled their approval and another couple of shots were fired harmlessly into the air. From somewhere, more whisky had appeared and was going from hand to hand, mouth to mouth.

'Pa,' said Vinnie, not looking directly at his father, 'don't let him talk to you like that.'

'Hush your mouth, child!' snapped his mother. And to her husband she said, 'Henry, pay that braggart no mind.'

But the man had already heard the pain in his son's voice and now he saw his face; his pride stung him to the quick. He pulled the barrel of the Sharps through the slit and slammed the wood back into place.

'Henry, don't! Don't pay them no heed!'

She tried to block his way, but he eased her aside, lifting the thick plank from the back of the door and reaching over to slide back the bolt.

'Henry!'

But he didn't hear her; all he could hear was Archibald's taunting. *Stinkin' yeller . . . wouldn't have the guts to look any son of mine in the face.* Without looking back, he stepped through into the yard. The strength of light made him blink. Someone ranged off to the left called a remark which he failed to hear clearly. He saw Archibald's mouth open wide, the dark red that was the inside of his mouth, the hollering laughter.

'Well, I'll be damned, Reb, if you ain't got a mite of spunk in you after all!'

Archibald shook his head, lifted the black felt hat clear and whooped it through the air. He pulled one of his pistols from his belt and shot Henry low in the chest.

The ball drove between the ribs, crashing Henry back against the door and sending it into the cabin with a vicious swing. One of Henry's arms struck the door jamb and he bounced awkwardly out towards the yard, blood already seeping through his shirt and the top of his workpants. As he reeled uncertainly four or five other shots sank into his body, most of the men with their guns drawn now and firing indiscriminately.

Vinnie ran from the back of the cabin, his moment of frozen terror broken by the fusillade of shots. His sister lunged at him and caught only air. At the last moment his mother's fingers caught his shirt collar and clung fast.

'March!' screamed the woman. 'The door! The door!'

But the girl's response was too slow, too late. The mother succeeded in dragging her son back into the room, finally pushing him against the table and only then turning away, trying to bring level the musket towards the door.

A boot lashed forward and kicked the door hard against the girl, splitting her left cheek like a beak breaking just-ripe fruit. The wooden bar clattered from her hands. Almost simultaneously, the musket was knocked upwards and then wrenched from the woman's hands. She turned and leaped at the table in one final effort to reach the handgun which lay there. Already seeing her daughter in the corner of her eye, needing to know where in the room she was so that the single shot she would have time to fire would not be wasted. Already asking her daughter's forgiveness . . .

An outflung leg sent her sprawling, knuckles cracking against the floor, the breath driven out of her by the speed and force of the fall. She tried to roll over and crawl but her head spun and somewhere at its centre was the scream of either a daughter or a son. Something bulked into her side, close by her kidneys and in spite of herself she was vomiting, tears blinding her eyes.

Everything was swallowed inside R.G. Archibald's laughter, the dark red roar of his mouth: everything but the first faint smell of burning.

They saw the grey spiral of smoke, slow against the flat sky, long before the stench of burning penetrated their nostrils. Hardin reined in his mount and stood tall in the stirrups, his mouth working soundlessly. Close by him, John Wesley watched his father's reactions, the chewing of the mouth that he recognized so clearly, the tautness of his father's muscular body beneath the shiny black of his preacher's suit. On their way back from the monthly circuit meeting in the sweaty, crowded tent, they had made a detour out to visit with their kin, John Wesley's aunt and uncle and his cousins, Vinnie and March.

Now John Wesley waited, watched, already tall for his twelve years, tall and beginning to thicken out. Already, quick-tempered and as like to end an argument with a blow as not. Like the time the year before when Pat Duggan had been teasing him back of the school building about Linda. The knife had been out of his pocket and into his hand before Duggan had the sense or the time to realize he'd gone too far. John Wesley's father had insisted on paying for the boy's medical expenses, had wielded the strap that hung behind the scullery door until his son's buttocks had been smeared with blood. Then he had stood over him and read from his leather-bound Bible while his wife bathed John Wesley's behind and listened to her husband's sonorous voice.

John Wesley had forgotten the pain, remembered the beating itself as some kind of trophy; he had neither heard nor learned the lesson.

Now he watched his father's stern face as the lines drew deeper and the eyes darkened. Without a word, Hardin kicked his spurs into his animal's flanks and set off at a gallop towards the smoke, John Wesley, excitement rising in his throat, following on behind as close as he could.

The preacher ordered his son to stay back some thirty yards from the smoking ruins, dismounting himself and walking slowly forward, pistol drawn and cocked. The stink of charred wood was tainted by the slightly sweet smell of what Hardin recognized all too readily as flesh. As he kicked his way through the debris, he discovered that his wife's bullet-ridden brother had been left, or thrown, close against the rear wall. One arm was badly burned and the skin at one side of his face was so scorched that it had begun to blacken and crack, breaking off like brittle, blistering paint.

The woman was face-down inside the corral, her skirt still high above her head and flapping, blood-spattered, in the breeze. Hardin knelt beside her and covered her legs, the invocation to a wrathful God loud enough on his lips for his son to hear and echo.

It was John Wesley who found his young cousin, Vinnie. Drawn by the soft cries of a small animal, he ignored his father's warning and followed the sounds to where the cat stood alongside Vinnie's head, lapping with delicate taste the blood that was drying in a cracked line that ran across the dry ground from the boy's smashed skull.

At least, reasoned Hardin later, that was better than his son discovering the girl where she had been hurled. Akimbo amongst the stumps of vegetables in her father's garden, March's stained and soiled body stared eyeless into the sun, a single feather caught between her arm and the recently turned earth.

They buried them behind the burned-out buildings, working without words, father and son, the hate simmering inside each of them only to be released by the preacher when he roared his funeral oration to a congregation of one.

For John Wesley Hardin, the rage was to find release three years later.

Two

Winter 1868

'Cold enough to freeze your balls off, ain't it, boy?'

John Wesley grinned across at his uncle and slapped his hands hard against the front of his plaid coat, shaking down a ripple of frost. 'Sure is, Uncle Aaron. That an' more.'

'Get us back to the house, we'll hunker down front of the fire with a shot of corn mash . . . how's that sound?'

'Pretty good,' John Wesley laughed.

Aaron settled his ham-like hand on his nephew's shoulder and gripped tight. He ran a mite wild at times, but for all that he was a good enough kid. Hell, kid! Already he weren't more than a couple of inches less than himself and he had good muscle on his limbs. Never run to fat, though, too much energy working itself off. Even when he weren't moving nothin' else his eyes were on the move an' times he chewed away at the inside of his mouth like his pa did.

'Don't imagine you get too much whisky come your way, do you, John? That brother of mine bein' a man of the cloth an' all.'

John Wesley shook his head. 'Pa takes a nip sometimes. If he leaves the bottle around, I'll sneak a swallow or two when he ain't lookin'.'

'Huh! Never let him catch you, boy, or he'll whip your ass from here to the Promised Land.'

John Wesley nodded. 'One time he did just that. Come in the house an' I was standing there with this bottle in my hand. Pulled it away and tried to get it round behind my back. Shakin' so much at him bein' there so sudden, like the devil himself or somethin', I was throwin' whisky all over the floor.'

Aaron laughed and slapped his belly. 'What in the Lord's name did your pa say about that?'

'Told me it was a sin to waste good liquor that ways. Then he held out his hand for the bottle, took a snap at it an' reached for the belt back of the door.'

'I bet he whipped you good,' laughed Aaron.

John Wesley shook his head from side to side, smiling at what distance had changed to an almost pleasant memory. 'He beat me till my ass was bluer'n my ma's blueberry pie.'

Aaron chortled fit to bust. 'Bluer'n blueberry pie, that's good, John. That's good.'

The excited breath of both of them stood out clear on the cold air.

'Blacker,' said John Wesley, aiming to go one better, 'blacker than the face of one these niggers you got workin' your fields.'

Aaron couldn't speak for shaking; his mouth was open and dark, his eyes running with tears that started to freeze up before they ran off his face. He clung to his nephew for support, controlling himself slowly. When eventually he could speak, he pulled John Wesley close and said: 'Them as killed your kin three year back, you known them for niggers, don't you?'

'Pa, he . . .'

'Black trash, sure as I stand here!'

'We never . . .'

'Who else d'you think would do a thing like that?' Aaron swung the youth round to face him, his breath ripe in John Wesley's face. 'Who else but niggers'd rape an' burn the way they done? What d'you think? What?'

John Wesley pulled himself free, stepped away, turned, a hand scooping hair back from his eyes and high across his forehead. 'Guess you got to be right.'

'Right?' boomed Aaron. 'Sure as all Hell I'm right. Didn't your pa tell you that? Didn't he tell you the truth of that, boy?'

John Wesley nodded. 'He allowed some of 'em was likely niggers . . .'

'Some! Likely! He ain't seein' things square an' true, that's for sure. He been starin' in that damned Bible of his till nothin' comes out right no more.'

'The way we heard it, Uncle Henry got to cussin' this feller in town. Northerner, but he was white. Ran loose with a bunch of fellers black an' white. They . . .'

But Aaron moved away from him, wide-eyed, both hands pushed out with their fingers spread. 'Hold on, now. You hold on one little minute, now. Let's be clear what you're sayin' here. Are you, are you accountin' that them folk of yours got what was comin' to 'em? That Henry deserved all that . . . all that filth on account of he gave some piece of carpetbaggin' trash a piece of his mind? Is . . . is that what you're sayin'?'

'No, Uncle Aaron, course I ain't.'

'That's all right then. Because if I thought you was . . .'

'What I was sayin' was that we, Pa an' me, we don't reckon the folks as did this was all black.'

Aaron stuck his finger close to his nephew's face and back of it, his own face, reddened and flushed, showed sweat despite the cold. 'They was runnin' with niggers, weren't they?'

'Sure, I . . .'

'Ridin' with 'em?'

'Yeah.'

'Likely livin' with 'em. Like they was the same, like they was equal?'

'Likely.'

'There y'are then. Live with a nigger, treat him as equal, you gets like 'em. They contaminate you. Deep down. Deep inside. Oh, on the surface you may look the same, you may look white, but you ain't. No, indeed. You ain't. Not any more, no. You're black. You're a nigger. And that . . . that's what did this to your kin. That's what raped that little cousin of yours an' her ma. Raped an' killed and burnt like animals on account of that's what they had become.'

He grasped John Wesley hard by both arms, fingers pressing deep through his own gloves and the thickness of the youth's coat.

'You see that, don't you, boy?'

John Wesley nodded, tight-lipped, trying not to react to the pain that was beginning to make itself felt in the muscles of his upper arms.

'You see that?'

'Sure.'

'You sure?'

'I said it, I see.'

'Okay. All right.' Aaron nodded once, breathing heavily. He loosed his grip and stepped away, holding the young man still with his eyes. 'Long as you know . . . niggers done it. You got that?'

John Wesley sighed. 'Sure. Niggers done it.'

Aaron's face broke into a smile, his mouth opened to a harsh laugh. He turned John Wesley towards the house, an arm across his shoulders. 'Let's get that drink.'

The following morning Aaron took one of the wagons out to the eastern quarter and left John Wesley to tend to the high barn with Little Billy for a companion. Billy was Aaron's son and so John Wesley's cousin. A year younger than John Wesley, he was gangling, uncoordinated and none too bright. The pair of them got on well enough, without ever being real friends. Like most youths of their age, they were forever trying to best one another, whether at riding, running, climbing or fighting.

Apart from riding, on account of the way Little Billy's body suddenly became controllable as soon as he sat in the saddle, John Wesley had to try hard not to win too easily.

They'd been sorting and cleaning tackle in the barn for no more than an hour when Billy curled a cinch strap over on to a bale of straw and cussed good and loud.

'What's eatin' you?' asked John Wesley.

'This work.'

'What about it?'

'It's borin'.'

'It ain't hard.'

Little Billy made a face and swung one of his long arms out to one side. 'I never said it was hard, I said it was borin'. I'm sick to my hind teeth with this blasted barn.'

John Wesley shook his head and grinned.

'Now what's eatin' you?' Billy snapped at him.

'Me? Nothin'.'

'Then take that fool grin off your face.'

John Wesley stood quite still and did exactly as his cousin told him; the only thing was, the look that replaced the grin was one to make Little Billy realize he'd opened his mouth a mite too wide and at least once too often. John Wesley's eyes narrowed and seemed to darken as the pupils contracted; his mouth began to work, the edge of the lower lip sucked in hard; the skin was tighter, whiter over the cheekbones.

'Hey, now! I didn't . . . I . . . you watch . . . there ain't no call . . .'

Little Billy stopped trying to talk his way out of trouble and decided to make a run for it. He turned too fast and his left foot skidded on some loose straw and he skittered several yards before tumbling on to one knee.

'Hey, now!'

Little Billy's arms swung up as John Wesley closed fast. They blocked the first two blows and deflected a third down on to his shoulder. Through the swirl of fists he could see the look of concentration on his cousin's face.

'John!'

But John Wesley was tired of punches that failed to land. He drew back from the crouching youth far enough to swing his boot hard under Little Billy's ribs. Billy went careening over, clutching his side and gasping for breath. He rolled and drew his legs up into his stomach. Tears sprang from his eyes.

'You bastard!' he called, anger fighting through despite himself.

John Wesley kicked him a second time, his boot burying into

the midst of the curled mass. A third followed. Then, before Little Billy could scream louder or struggle away, the blows ceased. For several seconds, Billy lay where he was, trying to control his breathing, pressing his bunched hands into the flesh where the boots had landed. He could hear John Wesley's breathing too, more controlled than his own, but signalling his exertion clearly enough. Billy waited until he was sure the attack was over. He looked over his arm and saw his cousin standing a dozen feet away, staring down at him with pity in his eyes.

Little Billy didn't want pity – but neither did he want to get beaten again.

'See now,' he began, pushing himself painfully to his feet, 'I didn't mean nothin' by it. What I called you an' all. How could I, John? I mean, us bein' kin an' all.'

Unable to stand quite straight, he advanced towards John Wesley gingerly, each step jarring his bruised body.

'Shake on it, huh?'

Little Billy extended his hand towards John Wesley, wincing a little as he did so.

'Friends, huh?' Billy said.

John Wesley moved slowly, his arm sliding towards Billy more like a snake than anything else. Little Billy shuddered but held his ground, the fingers of his outstretched hand shaking perceptibly.

A quick smile flicked over John Wesley's face. 'Sure, Billy,' he said. 'Friends.'

The handshake was fast, firm. Billy saw the smile back of his cousin's eyes and responded, almost in spite of himself.

'That's it, then,' sighed Little Billy with relief. 'We made up.'

'Yeah,' said John Wesley, grinning. 'That's it.'

He slid his hand clear, turned slickly away, moving towards his left. Midway through his turn, his body broke its movement almost imperceptibly. The direction reversed, faster now, and John Wesley's right arm flew out, the knuckles at the back of his hand striking the side of Little

Billy's face with a whiplash crack. Billy's head jolted back hard and a moment later it jerked forward again as John Wesley's other hand, fisted tight, drove into the pit of his stomach.

Spittle shot from Billy's open mouth, mucus from his nose. He gasped and overbalanced, falling forwards to the ground. Before he got there, John Wesley had reached down and caught him, one hand grasping the back of his shirt, the other tangled in Billy's unruly hair. He immediately began to swing Billy backwards and forwards, preparing to hurl him into the side wall with its collection of two-tined forks and toothed rakes. Billy's shouts echoed through the barn.

John Wesley swung and laughed, laughed and swung.

'No! No! Don't!'

John Wesley's laughter grew as Billy's protests were drowned in a splutter of his own snot and vomit.

One more swing and . . .

One more and there was a black standing in the doorway to the barn; he was naked to the waist, despite the bitter cold outside. His right hand gripped a scythe tight across in front of his bare chest.

'You best let the boy go.'

Astounded, John Wesley opened his hands and Little Billy fell to the barn floor with a thump. Billy whimpered and curled into himself again before starting slowly to crawl away towards the bales of straw.

'Who the hell d'you think you are?' asked John Wesley, biting down on his anger, his voice low and cold.

The black looked back at him with a hint too much boldness for John Wesley's liking. 'I works for Mister Aaron.'

'I said, who the hell are you?'

'I'm Mage.'

'You're interferin' where you ain't got no business,' said John Wesley, his voice sharpening, moving himself gradually closer.

Mage tapped the sharp curve of the scythe against the fingers of his left hand. 'I was lookin' after Mister Aaron's boy.'

John Wesley snorted, his face incredulous. 'Shift your ass out of here!'

'Not till you let that boy alone.'

Over by the straw bales, Little Billy moaned and sniffed.

John Wesley rushed at the black, watching the vicious-looking scythe closely despite his anger. He saw Mage's arm begin to curl back and dipped his body into a sideways curve that was set to take him underneath the implement's swing. He judged it more or less right. The handle end jarred against the top edge of his left shoulder and made him grit his teeth to stop from calling out. The sharpened blade slashed the air several inches above his head and as it passed, John Wesley slammed his fist into Mage's ribs catching him beneath the heart. The black staggered backwards but by no more than a few paces. The scythe was still in his hand.

John Wesley rubbed at his shoulder automatically, immediately angry with himself for showing even that much sign of weakness. He moved towards Mage, cautiously, slowly now, watching the weapon, watching the man's face. Back of the pair of them, Little Billy stumbled to his feet and promptly sat back down on one of the bales, one hand pressed against the side of his face, the other rubbing his stomach.

'Back off now,' said Mage. 'You let me be.'

John Wesley smiled. 'Scared, nigger? That it? Scared now?'

'I ain't scared. Not of you, I ain't.'

'Huh! You're yeller right enough. Under that black skin you're piss-yeller!'

Mage's eyes widened and his fingers readjusted round the grip of the scythe; the end of his tongue pushed between his lips as he fought to contain his temper. There was nothing he would like more than to let that scythe have a real fine swing so it cleaved the head of that jumped-up white trash clean from his neck.

But Mage had lived long enough to know the consequences of such an action. And hard as his master was, bigoted as he was, at least he paid a high enough wage for Mage to eat and live half-way decent. At least he allowed him to get on with his work in his own way and his own time, just so long as Mage was occupied doing something from sun-up to sundown.

As for Little Billy over there, he was a good enough kid, considering that he was white. He surely didn't deserve to have his brains dashed out against no barn wall just 'cause some uppity bully took a fancy to it.

'C'mon, you yeller bastard!' John Wesley taunted him, his anger turning now to a bitter frustration. 'Set down that thing an' fight!'

Mage shook his head and began to back off, out through the barn door and into the yard beyond. John Wesley followed hard upon him, his eyes twitching and his teeth biting down against the inside of his mouth.

'You best go back in there an' see to that boy,' said Mage, 'he might've bust somethin' bad.'

John Wesley's fist jutted out fast. 'Who the hell you think you're tellin' what to do? Huh, nigger? Huh, trash? You tellin' me what to do?' He swung his left arm and pointed behind him. 'You're so all-fired concerned, you get your ass in there an' play doctor!'

Mage shrugged and turned his back, walking away fast, knowing that arguing further was a waste of time. John Wesley launched himself forward, one hand going for Mage's right arm, the other driving against the back of his neck.

The black went jolting forwards, his knees beginning to buckle beneath him. As he felt himself being forced down, he accentuated the fall, throwing his hip and tossing his attacker off to the side. John Wesley's fingers lost their grip and he went sliding away, landing with an awkward thump that raised a cloud of thick dust. Through the dust he saw the glint of the scythe.

The crack of pistol fire stopped all movement. Mage caught his breath, slowly turned his head to see his employer standing between barn and corral, his Colt Navy extended at arm's length in front of him. A little smoke still drifted up from the barrel.

The scythe fell between Mage's fingers and curved flatly on the ground.

John Wesley pushed himself up, turned, and began to walk towards the water trough.

Inside the barn, Little Billy was still sitting with his head between his knees, still trying to stop himself from vomiting through his hands.

Three

Aaron mulched the last vestiges of flavour from the remnants of his chewing tobacco and spat the plug into the fire. Flames hissed up and crackled and a thin spiral of soft grey smoke avoided the breast of the chimney and filtered out into the room.

Aaron glanced across at John Wesley, seated at the hefty rectangular table, sniffed the air, clapped his hands together and headed for the whisky bottle.

'Here!' The offer was more like a blow.

John Wesley hesitated only a moment, then took the tumbler from his uncle's hand.

Aaron swallowed half the contents of his own glass quickly and set it down on the table with a smack that was likely to break glass and table both.

'Damn!' he boomed. 'Damn!'

His fat finger wobbled a few inches off his nephew's face.

'Damn!'

The finger pulled back into a fist, the fist threatened then unfolded. Aaron turned bulkily away, stalked across the room, pulled the door open only to slam it shut, drank the remainder of his whisky and refilled the glass too fast, the liquor splashing over on to the floor.

'Boy, your pa warned me you might be trouble. He said you had a temper and a half brung you by some devil, but I never known it was goin' to be like this.'

John Wesley half rose from the chair. 'He was just a ni . . .'

'I ain't talkin' 'bout no nigger, I'm talkin' 'bout my boy.'

John Wesley sat back down. 'That weren't no more than a bit of fun.'

Aaron lunged at him, knocking the table sideways with his hip. He caught hold of the youth's shoulder and spun him round so hard that the chair went skidding away and John Wesley was left sitting on nothing.

'Fun! He's back in his room with a couple of ribs strapped up tight and there's three teeth missin' from his head.' He shook his nephew hard and let go like he was touching something that wasn't quite clean. 'If that's your idea of fun, there's somethin' strange about you that I don't understand.'

He stood clear, reaching in his pocket for some tobacco. 'Don't want to understand.' He bit off a chunk and began chomping down on it hard, getting it soft and pliable.

'An' as for Mage, hell, you know what I feel about niggers well as I do. But Mage's been workin' for me since he was younger'n you. He ain't never talked back, ain't never moaned about his work the way most of them idle bastards does. He's been cursin' me for a slave-drivin' white bastard under his breath all the time, only natural, but he ain't never showed it. What he did back at the barn maybe saved Little Billy's life.'

'That weren't . . .' John Wesley began, but his uncle cut him off angrily.

'Hold your tongue, boy! Hear me out. I've had to have that nigger whipped and now I've had to throw him off the place. I ain't goin' to get another one'll work like him.' The finger pointed squarely at John Wesley. 'You cost me, boy. You cost me in all kinds of ways, you understand that?'

John Wesley turned away from his uncle and stood close by the window, aimlessly watching the horses shifting places in the corral. His uncle's words spilled about him and he knew that all he had to do was wait for them to subside and stop and it would be over. There wasn't any point to answering back. As for that dumb nigger, well, he'd got what was coming to him. He only wished he'd been able to see the stockwhip being laid across his back till Mage started hollering for it to quit.

He didn't understand what his uncle was so mad about – hadn't he been the one tellin' him that it was niggers killed his kin and raped their womenfolk? And weren't all niggers alike? Ruinin' the whole damn state if folk was weak enough to give 'em the chance.

John Wesley's mouth ground tight. He'd reckoned his uncle as being strong enough to keep the blacks in their place. Now maybe he was finding out he'd judged him wrong. The youth's hands made themselves into fists. The threats and warnings sputtered into silence behind him, he heard heavy footsteps and anticipated the slam of the door.

Alone, the fists remained clenched, John Wesley's resolve became a vow.

John Wesley Hardin had been presented with his .44 pistol when he had been no more than eight years of age. To fight the good fight, his preacher father had admonished him. To carry on the crusade against the forces of the devil. As soon as the sermon had ended, he had taken his growing son clear of the house and begun teaching him to load and prime the weapon, getting the charges tamped down into place firmly. Then, two-handed, had come the first attempts to use the weapon accurately. There had been targets tacked to the side of the barn, bottles and cans first set along the uneven length of the fence and later hurled high into the air, the circular tops of cans sent skimming over the cold blue water of the creek.

When John Wesley's mother had queried whether her son should be spending so much time learning to use a gun instead of a plough, her husband had explained the necessity of both. It was, he said, an evil world – a world inhabited by sinners and the only way to walk through it with your head held high was to have a gun in one hand and a Bible in the other.

John Wesley sort of forgot about the Bible.

Not the .44.

He had it with him the day after his fight with Little Billy and his run-in with Mage; the day following Mage's beating and dismissal and his own dressing-down by his Uncle Aaron.

'You watch out,' Little Billy had told him in a low voice, 'that Mage, he's going to get even with you. He told me so.'

John Wesley had glanced at Billy and seen from the expression in his cousin's face that Billy wouldn't be any too sad if he did. But John Wesley carried on saddling his horse and paid the warning no mind – other than to make good and certain that his pistol was loaded and laying on top of the slicker he carried in his saddle bag.

He had no special idea where he was heading, simply wanted to get clear from the place for a few hours, away from Aaron's hostile eye. He figured it would all blow over soon enough if him and his uncle steered a wide berth around one another. So he rode towards the foothills that spread along the eastern edge of the trail to town. They pushed up, one above the other, like layers of some grandly designed wedding cake that had since begun to sag and decay. The upper ridges were iced with frost and unwelcoming. Back of them the clear sky was hung with tatters of darkening cloud.

John Wesley was wearing a short wool coat, his hat held tight beneath his chin with fastened cord and a brown scarf tied about his neck. Scuffed leather gloves kept the blood circulating through his fingers. The rounded plumes of his mount's breath rose on the wind and merged with his own before dispersing.

He circled around the small settlement of Moscow, turning in from the north past the wooden markers of the cemetery. His shout and the angry flap of his arms sent half a dozen large crows into the air from where they had been perched above the white-fringed headboards. A fine spray of frost fell over the graves as the birds worked their wide, lazy wings and made slow circles over John Wesley's head.

He cursed them and rode on towards the saloon and dining

room. A mug of hot coffee and a wedge of luke-warm pie prepared him for his return journey. The rowels of his spurs jangled discordantly as he strode out towards the hitching rail. The saddle creaked a little as he settled on to the horse's back. He retied the scarf, pulled his gloves from where he had tucked them in his belt, and on to his hands. One pat at the bulk of the .44 in the right-side saddle bag and he was on his way.

The road out of Moscow became a straggle of shacks whose walls and roofs were nailed together from oddments and sawn-off planks of wood, scraps of tin and copious quantities of sacking. A tent sagged against the wind. John Wesley pulled down the brim of his hat and readjusted his scarf so that it covered the lower half of his face. The road was bare to his right now, the few dwellings on the other side spread further and further apart.

A sandy-haired dog ran out from behind a short length of fence that didn't seem to be protecting anything other than itself. The dog yapped in front of John Wesley's horse and the animal shied away, the youth controlling it easily enough, shouting at the dog and making it bark all the louder. He brought the horse round on a short rein and drove it towards the dog, which went into a yowling cringe, hair bristling, before scampering back towards the fence with a fading succession of growls.

'Damn hound!' called John Wesley over his shoulder. 'Should've put a bullet through your head!'

He was so intent upon looking back that he failed at first to see Mage step out from the cover of the last shanty on the road. It took the black's angry voice to make the youth aware of his presence.

'You an' me, we got business, boy!'

The words spun through John Wesley's head without his hearing them clearly, though the tone was enough. Mage stood some fifteen yards down the road, a faded red shirt hanging out over his dark pants, his feet bare. His broad face stared angrily up at John Wesley and in place of the scythe from their previous meeting, a hefty, knotted stick was being tapped into the palm of Mage's left hand.

John Wesley looked back in disbelief, recalling Little Billy's words but still surprised that the black should dare to confront him.

'Business, boy!'

Mage gave the stick more air and thwacked it down into his hand hard.

'You owe me! You owe me plenty!'

John Wesley's mount shifted off to the side and he pulled it back round. His mouth was beginning to work greedily and his eyes were narrowing down as the black took half a dozen paces towards him.

'Get your ass down off that horse!'

John Wesley's sole answer was a slow sideways shake of his young head.

'I said, get down!' shouted Mage and made a short run forward, only stopping when he was close enough to seize hold of the bridle of the white youth's mount.

'You lost me my job, boy, an' got me whupped. Now I'm goin' to whup you!'

John Wesley leaned back in the saddle and Mage raised the stick towards him.

'Who's yeller now, boy?'

John Wesley turned his body away from the hefty weapon and Mage allowed himself a grim laugh that froze across his face when the youth came back round fast and with a pistol tight in his hand.

'You ain't . . .' Mage began, letting go of the bridle.

'Never knew I had this, did you?' said the smiling John Wesley. 'Never knew I was ridin' armed.'

Mage looked into John Wesley's face to see what he was going to do and right off knew the answer. He jumped back in with his stick swinging and John Wesley bit down inside his lower lip and fired into the black's face.

The explosion rocked and startled the horse, which reared up on its hind legs and almost unseated John Wesley from the saddle. He grasped the reins tightly in his left hand and pulled them against his chest, gripping the animal's flanks hard with his knees.

Mage, meanwhile, had staggered back, temporarily blinded, his face a mask of blood. He fell sideways, dropping the stick as he pushed out a hand to break his fall. He opened his mouth to cry out and immediately it filled with blood. Choking, coughing, Mage wiped at his face with his arm, screaming as the material of his shirt scraped across the torn opening of his wound.

John Wesley fought his horse under control and walked it slowly up to where Mage was now on his hands and knees, crawling blindly along, hands seemingly searching for his stick.

The .44 was still in John Wesley's right hand.

Twenty yards back along the road, the sandy dog was back on its rear legs, hair bristling, barking at a fast staccato. Further towards town, men and women were cautiously appearing, several of them taking the first tentative steps towards the incident.

Mage's fingers smeared themselves around the clumsy wooden stick and with a loud shout of pain and anger he thrust himself to his feet. Blood blinked away from his eyes, only to be replaced as more welled up from the bullet hole beneath them where Mage's cheek and half of his nose had been blasted away.

Bone showed through shredded flesh and skin.

The black's mouth let out a wordless shout and he stumbled in the direction of the horse.

John Wesley's arm came level and his thumb brought back the hammer of the gun.

March's stained and soiled body stared eyeless into the sun.

The pistol seemed to go off by itself. Mage was swung round as the slug tore into his right shoulder and he dropped the stick for a second time. For a second time he staggered away before falling.

John Wesley could hear folk shouting now and the sound of feet running towards him. He struggled with the reins, one-handed. Mage shifted his weight on to his left arm and tried to crawl forward. Blood ran easily out of his wounds, too warm for the clotting cold.

That's what did this to your kin. Raped an' killed and burnt...

Mage clawed the air with his hand and thrust his blood-strewn face up towards the white youth, the mouth open in a dreadful scream.

Deep down. They contaminate you. Deep down.

John Wesley bit down inside the soft flesh of his mouth until it bled. He squinted along the barrel of his pistol and fired into the centre of the yelling, dying mass that was Mage. Then, with men shouting close by yet hesitating to come too close for fear the youth might run amok and turn his gun upon them, John Wesley wheeled his mount through a wide circle and kicked his spurs hard against its sides.

Mage collapsed into the dust, at least half of those watching already telling themselves that he'd got what was coming to him. By the time John Wesley was out of sight, there was no one around to watch the final twitches of the black's life. When the last convulsion was over, the sandy-haired dog came sniffing suspiciously round and planted a couple of wet licks by the side of the dead man's ear. After that, he lifted his leg, peed over Mage's leg and trotted happily away.

The men who finally came to lift the black's body away did so out of a sense of duty to the community rather than any respect for the deceased. After all, as the leader of the council pointed out, even in this weather a body gets to stink sooner or later and once the jackals and vultures began tearing strips off him, well, it wouldn't be nice for the womenfolk to see things like that.

So three of them dragged him off the road inside a length of sacking and carried him fifty yards beyond the town limits before digging a deep enough grave to ensure he wouldn't get dug up again by the first hungry creature that happened along. They wandered back towards the saloon, thirsty enough to drink down the few dollars they'd been paid and were surprised to hear some of the inhabitants actually suggesting that black or no, what had taken place that day was still murder.

'Damn me,' said one of the gravediggers over his beer, 'if somethin' like this don't bring all the nigger-lovers out of the woodwork like lice.'

His companions nodded in agreement and got back to their drinking.

Aaron and Little Billy were on their way back home after spending the best part of the day mending fences and arguing. The flat-bed wagon bounced back of the two-horse team, Aaron alternately chewing and spitting tobacco as he drove. Billy's fingers were sore from work, callouses not yet strong enough to protect his skin from blisters. He tried to avoid his father's eye, not wishing to be told again how he'd let him down in failing to stand up to his cousin better than he did. His father didn't understand the nature of his cousin's temper, that was part of the problem. If he'd seen his face it might have been different.

'Why don't you send him off with his tail between his legs, pa?' Billy had asked.

'Because he's kin,' his father had growled back. 'Close kin at that. An' a man has a duty to look after his own.'

That hadn't allowed much argument, so Little Billy had kept to himself the thought that it would have been better to have kept Mage and got rid of John Wesley.

A couple of miles out, a rider hailed them with a wave of his stetson and Aaron began to rein in the horses. Harry Jefferson, setting off for his own place to the west, was a bundle of old clothes seated on a shaggy mule, his unkempt beard wrapped around the stem of his upside-down clay pipe like a filthy scarf.

'Jesus, pa,' exclaimed Billy, 'what you stoppin' for? He stinks worse'n four-day-old horse shit!'

Aaron let go the rein long enough to give his son a backhander across the face. 'Shut your mouth or wash it out! You remember who you're talking to.'

Little Billy cringed back and choked down a cry, the cold making his face smart all the more. His small fists clenched tight against his legs and as he stared at the ground he wished he had the guts to drive them hard into his father's back. One day, maybe he would.

'Harry!' called Aaron in greeting.

Harry Jefferson wiped his running nose with the back of a woollen glove, sniffed, nodded, cleared his throat, considered spitting but finally swallowed instead. 'Heard 'bout the shootin'?'

Aaron shook his head. 'What shootin'?'

'Out Moscow way.'

'Uh-uh.' Aaron shook his head again and wished Jefferson would shift either himself or his mule down wind a little.

Harry Jefferson pushed his hand against his nose and rubbed vigorously. 'Kin of yours, ain't he?'

'Who?' Aaron leaned forward, regarded the man with real interest for the first time.

'That kid you got out at your place – he's a Hardin, ain't he?'

'He is.'

'Well, he got himself a man today.'

'What man? What in God's name you runnin' off at the mouth about?'

Jefferson gave a gruff laugh that broke into a cough. 'That black you had workin' for you.'

'Mage?'

'Huh?'

'I said, Mage.'

'If that was his name.'

Aaron pointed a finger at Jefferson and said, 'What the hell happened?'

'Shot him, that's what.'

'Who says so?'

'Most everyone,' Jefferson grunted. 'Half Moscow seen it go down. Emptied a .44 into him and rode off leavin' him for dead.'

'Jesus Christ!'

'Yes, sir,' smiled Harry Jefferson lopsidedly, 'that's where he's gone. Just another nigger with wings an' a harp.'

But Aaron had stopped listening. He let out the brake and whipped up the horses and headed home as fast as he could, Little Billy struggling to keep the smile he felt inside from welling up on to his face; struggling to keep from telling his father, I told you so.

It wasn't two days before Aaron got word that some of the council in Moscow had felt it their bounden duty to report the killing to the nearest army post and that the officer in charge had responded by offering to send a small detachment into the community in an attempt to apprehend the murderer.

As soon as Aaron heard this he bundled the protesting John Wesley on to a horse and took him towards Sumpter where good friends of his had a small farm. In addition to being friends, the McCandleses were known sympathizers for the late Confederate cause and likely to look kindly on a youngster who'd got himself into trouble with the Federal troops for shooting a black.

Sure enough, Jamie and Beth McCandles greeted John Wesley like he was some kind of hero and promised to hide him and look out for him until the chase died down and it was safe to return to his uncle's. John Wesley enjoyed his new-found status and was soon giving embroidered accounts of the shooting to the McCandles children and then to any passer-by who just happened to stop by to catch a glimpse of the youth who'd single-handedly put paid to one of them worthless blacks.

'Only shame of it is,' Jamie McCandles announced to a dozen or more friends who'd foregathered one Friday night and who'd been toasting the young gunman liberally, 'it took a youngster like Hardin here to show others the way.'

A cheer rose brokenly up and John Wesley fidgeted some, feeling pleased with himself nonetheless.

'The way things are going down here since the war, we got to watch out we don't all get run under by a bunch of nigra-lovers and carpet-baggers out for all they can get. Every which way you turn there's some Unionist banker lookin' to get one man's land under a mortgage or foreclose someone else's. There's blacks who spent their whole lives till now as slaves marchin' around the streets all spruced up like they was takin' over. And if a man tries to do something about the state of things, if he stands up an' lets himself be counted, the way Hardin here done, well, either the Union army or the state police force slaps him down.'

'That's right!' called out someone in support.

'You said it!' shouted another.

'And remember,' said a voice from the side of the room, 'that police force you're talkin' about, that's blacks an' whites ridin' together. I ask you – what kind of police force is that?'

So the jug was passed round again from hand to hand and pretty soon Confederate songs were being sung and Beth McCandles disappeared into the loft and returned with the flag of the Confederacy, which she unveiled and draped over the table with great cheering and one or two drunken tears.

Young John Wesley took his share at the jug and listened to the rhetoric and reasoned that yes, he'd been right to shoot down Mage the way he had and given half the chance he'd do it again. These men gathered about him were decent and honest and they wouldn't let him get taken by whatever army patrols might be out looking for him. He felt safe and he felt that he was among his own kind, his own people . . . maybe more kin than his own father and mother. At least they didn't quote the good book at him every other minute of the day.

A gun in one hand and a Bible in the other, his father had said. All right. But here were the McCandleses and plenty more like them, who were like to throw down that Bible and take up a second gun instead.

'John!' The voice was low and urgent, a hand shaking him by the shoulder. 'John! Wake up!'

He jerked into a sitting position, his right hand reaching out towards the pistol stashed below his pillow. There was little light in the barn, no more than a faint square that filtered through the sacking nailed to the opening in the roof. John Wesley was annoyed with himself that he had been sleeping so soundly as to allow McCandles to climb the ladder and get so close before he woke.

'What is it?'

'It's all right,' said McCandles, stopping the youth's hand at the pillow. 'They're ten miles or more from here. They spent the night in lodgings in Sumpter and now they're fixing to ride south-west.'

'How d'you know this?'

McCandles smiled in the almost-dark. 'I've got friends in Sumpter – we've got friends there. Those who think like us about what's happening to Texas.'

John Wesley had all but ceased to listen. He was out from under his blanket and pulling on his boots. The cold smacked him hard and he grabbed for his pants and vest, eager to be fully dressed and away.

'You don't understand,' said McCandles, 'they'll swing wide of here for certain. You're safe for now.'

John Wesley looked at him, his features gradually sharpening. 'And later?'

'If they head back this way we'll have warning in plenty of time.'

John Wesley shook his head, climbed into his thick wool coat. 'It's not good enough.'

An expression of some disappointment came over Jamie McCandles' face. 'You'll be running then?'

John Wesley had hold of the front of McCandles' coat so fast that the startled farmer was almost pitched back from the loft floor. 'Who said anythin' about runnin'?'

'I . . .'

'Who?'

'I thought . . .'

'I ain't runnin'. I just don't want to spend all my time cooped up here, shufflin' around under straw like some rat, while a handful of soldiers ride around the country lookin' for me.'

McCandles nodded. 'What you fixin' to do, John?'

John Wesley looked at him straight. 'How many are there of 'em?'

'Three.'

'Three!' repeated the youth, incredulous. 'Is that all?'

McCandles nodded.

'Okay.' John Wesley moved past him and began to descend the ladder, the farmer following. On the ground, Hardin pointed towards the stalls. 'You lend me a fast horse. Fast an' strong.'

McCandles agreed readily, still not certain of what the young man had in mind.

'That and that double-barrel shotgun you got up at the house. I'm fixin' to let those army boys find me sooner than they think.'

Jamie McCandles' eyes widened and then he nodded slowly, setting off towards the house to fetch the youth what he wanted. 'You want breakfast before you ride?' he called over his shoulder.

John Wesley shook his head. 'I'll wait till I get back, then I'll be obliged for a steak and a batch of eggs. A mornin's huntin's like to give me an appetite.'

The water running along the creek bottom was sparkling cold; it took the blue of the sky and froze it to sapphire. The bared sun hung in it like a worked nugget of pure gold. Branches of the few trees were lined with frost along their upper edges. Scrub close to an outcrop of rock was dappled white. John Wesley's breath rolled through the morning air, his hands fought for warmth inside the gloves they wore. Even through the leather, the metal of the shotgun barrel was like ice.

Away on both sides of the creek, the road from Sumpter was a flattened line through the hard land.

John Wesley's wind caught in his throat when he saw the three riders upon it, too far distant even to make out their uniforms. His mouth was cold and dry and his stomach rolled and hollowed out. A nervous hand reached between the folds of his buttoned top coat and touched the butt of his .44. He angled the shotgun round so that it rested close to the pommel of the saddle. Backing the horse up towards rock and trees, he could see the blue of the uniform, then the yellow stripe markings. Three men, troopers. Searching for him.

The youth turned the horse through a circle and satisfied himself that he could not be seen.

Within minutes he could hear the rise and fall of their voices, see the dark beard of the one at the centre, recognize the corporal's stripes on his uniform. Occasional words, phrases strung themselves clear above the cold singing of the water. John Wesley sucked in his cheeks and reached forward to stroke the horse on its broad nose, sensing the warmth of the animal's blood beneath the cold hair of its coat.

They were no more than fifty yards off and he could see each face clearly, the two at either side of the corporal so young, not many years older than himself, if at all. Cold wrenched at their faces and wrinkled them like apples kept over-long at the back of a drawer.

'. . . blasted cold . . .'

The shotgun rested across the fold of John Wesley's left arm, the trigger finger of his right hand easy inside the guard. The soldiers hesitated at the far side of the creek, two of them allowing their mounts to dip their heads and drink.

John Wesley was certain that they must hear the sound of his breathing, but they did not seem to look in his direction once.

'C'mon.' The corporal flicked the reins and started off into the water.

John Wesley's tongue shifted between his lips and tiny bubbles of moisture remained in its track and froze there.

The other men grudgingly followed on close behind.

John Wesley kicked his horse from hiding.

The three men swung their heads round, startled, only the corporal making the instinctive move towards the pistol holstered at his side. John Wesley squeezed back on both barrels and the long shotgun leapt and blurted 10 gauge shot. The bearded face of the corporal was lashed and shredded almost to the bone; his neck opened like soft fruit and blood poured instantly over the front of his uniform. Alongside him, one of the young troopers took the remainder of the shot in cheek and eye, shoulder and chest.

John Wesley saw the blood, the expressions of surprise and pain that stared through it; saw all this and yet wondered if he had hit them at all. Both men hung in their saddles for what seemed to the youth a long, long time. Then, first the trooper, finally the corporal, swayed and tumbled sideways and hit the water with a parallel splash. Instantly, the creek was stained red. Blue uniform limbs thrashed vainly, as if belonging to children who had never learnt to swim.

The third trooper and John Wesley stared at one another, the trooper gazing at the shotgun, knowing that both barrels had been emptied, seeing no other gun. His own fingers fumbled with the flap of his holster, but his gloves were too large and difficult to control; the button on the flap was stiff and unyielding.

'You lookin' for John Wesley Hardin?'

The trooper shucked off his glove and pulled the holster open, touched the hard coldness of the butt.

The shotgun was now in the youth's left hand.

The corporal seemed to be sitting up in the water, his beard smeared and specked with red, his face ripped and dead.

'Well, you found him!'

The .44 came out of John Wesley's coat and his arm extended past the horse's head. The trooper's hands wouldn't work, wouldn't obey him, wouldn't finally pull the gun clear.

John Wesley's head jerked aside as the corporal collapsed on to his side with a heavy splash. When he looked back, the trooper's pistol was in his hand. John Wesley had another moment of disbelief, hesitation. Screwing up his eyes, the young trooper fired; John Wesley felt something tug hard at his left sleeve and he almost dropped the shotgun from his grasp. Instead, he raised the .44 a couple of inches and fired twice in rapid succession; he opened his mouth wide and fired once more. The trooper rolled off the back of his mount, which, relieved of its burden, trotted across the stream and some twenty yards down the empty road.

John Wesley tucked the .44 back inside his coat and shifted the shotgun back to his right hand. He gave the bloodied creek a final glance and set off towards the McCandles place at a fierce gallop.

'You got to get out of here, John,' Jamie McCandles all but yelled. 'It ain't no good your stayin' here now.'

John Wesley stared at the man, anger in every curve and line of his young face. 'You knew what I was going to do. You good as told me to get on and do it.'

'That ain't true!'

'No?' John Wesley hurled the long-barrelled shotgun across the space between them. 'Then what in the Lord's name d'you give me that for? You reckon I was headin' down that creek fishin' with it?'

McCandles hung his head and said nothing; right then there didn't seem to be anything else he could say. His wife came forward and touched him lightly on the arm, wiping stray hairs away from her eyes with her other hand.

'Jamie's right,' she said to the young man. 'When the army realizes those three ain't comin' back they'll comb this area like they was panning for gold. If you don't move on, and now, you'll be dead before your sixteenth birthday.' She glanced at her husband. 'And others along with you.'

Letting go of McCandles she stepped closer to John Wesley. 'John, we ain't sayin' you done wrong. You know what we think about that. But killing three troopers like that, it's going to make it difficult round these parts for a lot of us for a long time. But we'll do what we can. There's hot food and coffee inside and I'll make you up a sack of supplies. Ammunition, too. We'll give you the names of some good Confederate friends across the state who'll look out for you. And while you're gettin' ready, Jamie'll ride back out to the creek and get rid of them bodies.'

McCandles nodded. 'That's right. I'll pick up a couple of the men as was here the other night to give me a hand. We'll bury 'em and make 'em harder to find. Cover any tracks we can. You just cut and run as soon as you're ready. You're goin' to be doin' a whole lot of that from here on in.'

John Wesley stilled the slightest tremors at the side of his face. He acknowledged McCandles and followed his wife over towards the house. McCandles' words jiggled through his brain as he walked: ... *cut and run soon as you're ready. You're goin' to be doin' a whole lot of that from here on in. A whole lot of that*.

The coffee was black and bitter and the slice of pie that Beth McCandles cut for him was stodgy and stuck in his throat.

Four

Spring 1874
Comanche County, Texas

Governor Davis hadn't taken to the idea of reforming the Texas Rangers; he preferred his mixed-race state police and county sheriffs and deputies, most of whom were at least half-way loyal to his office and were happy enough to go along with his ideas about reconstruction. But the lawless elements were getting more obviously out of hand and the northern and southern borders of the state were particularly notorious for harbouring desperadoes of every persuasion and proclivity. Open and often lethal rivalry between the big cattlemen was another major cause for concern.

There were times when the Sutton–Taylor feud, for instance, threatened to draw the whole of both DeWitt and Gonzales Counties, Comanche County too, into what amounted to a running battle. The families had brought the feud with them from the Carolinas and here they had more space and more money to carry on their fight. Both sides employed as many men on account of the way they handled a gun as for how they could ride a bronc, or rope and brand a steer. Among Sutton's cohorts was Shanghai Pierce, a cattleman who stood close to six and a half feet and had served as regimental butcher in the First Texas Cavalry during the War Between the States. Pierce had built up a herd of his own by branding strays and any other steers that chanced to drift in his direction. Many of Sutton's other supporters were officially upholders of the law, such as Charles Webb, who was a deputy sheriff of Comanche County, and Jack Helm, who was both sheriff of DeWitt County and a captain of the state police.

The Taylor faction was not strong on peace officers – what they did enjoy was the support of the Clements family, Mannen and his brothers Jim, Joseph and Gyp, to say nothing of the Clements' cousin, John Wesley Hardin.

Things had got to the point where Governor Davis was being bombarded by advice from both friends and enemies to get to grips with the situation before it ruined his chances of re-election. Davis hummed and hawed and got as far as issuing instructions that the feasibility of the Rangers being reactivated on a limited and strictly controlled scale be examined by the state legislature.

In the event, his moves were too half-hearted either to save his own political future or diminish the violence of the Sutton–Taylor feud. He was swept out of office and replaced by Richard Coke, who read through the reports his predecessor had prepared and immediately gave orders that the Texas Rangers be reinstated in order to deal with what was an extremely dangerous situation and to balance the bias and inefficiency of many of the state police.

So it was that the call went out to men who were strong-willed and strong-bodied, better than most with horse or gun, both able to act under their own initiative and under orders. Men who, as far as the word could mean anything in that territory in the eighteen-seventies, were men of honour. There were four of them in the deputy sheriff's office in Comanche late this particular afternoon, gathered there to listen to Charlie Webb and Marvin Peake tell their version of events that had taken place the preceding year.

The most outstanding of these four Texas Rangers, as far as appearance went, was Lefty O'Neal. In most company, O'Neal's height might have been enough to mark him out since he stood seven inches above six feet, a couple of inches more than the renowned Shanghai Pierce. The majority of folk would have noticed him for his moustache which changed colour several shades along its length, ranging from dark brown through a gingery red to almost white, and which drooped several inches on either side of his mouth. Yet it was for neither of those features that Lefty was most known – the feature those who saw him remembered best and talked about was his head. High-domed, bald save for a sprinkling of brown hair above the ears, its crown was decorated by a spreading blue tattoo which incorporated a wide-branching tree, several varieties of flower, some intertwined snakes and the word Martha.

Very few men ever plucked up the courage to give their curiosity full rein and ask Lefty the origins of his strange dome. He wasn't the kind of man whose manner encouraged conversation to flow fast and loose. Indeed, the only ones who ever mentioned the tattoo at all were very drunk when they did so and usually very unconscious almost immediately afterwards. So far no one, drunk or sober, had asked him who Martha might be or have been. It was information that he never volunteered.

Nor was it clear why he had been given his nickname, since it didn't apply to any of his prominent features. He wasn't even left-handed, rather he was ambidextrous and one of the few men for whom wearing twin pistols was more than show.

Lefty was sitting in one of the deputy's straight-backed chairs, his length somehow wound about it and making the chair look woefully inadequate. Lamar stood close at Lefty's back, leaning against the side wall. He was a heavily-bearded man with broad shoulders and a thick neck that was marked indelibly at the left side and over the Adam's apple with rope burns that shone scarlet when his anger was aroused.

Keogh would have been reckoned tall in other company than Lefty O'Neal's. He was slender in build, his fingers toyed with an unlit cigarette as he straddled a chair that was set close to the centre of the room. His face was round and far younger than his years, made strange by the oriental cast of his eyes, green-hued and set at a definite slant.

In contrast to Keogh's automatically nervous actions, the fourth Ranger was the stillest of the group. Wes Hart was wiry with the impression of a man whose considerable strength was very much under control. The cheek bones of his lean face were prominent and high, pushing the tanned skin taut beneath eyes of faded blue that seemed to see everything without ever moving. His brown hair hung loose to the crumpled collar of his dark blue shirt. A faint moustache grew from the stubble about his mouth and over his angled jaw that stubble was almost a beard. Hart wore a plain leather waistcoat over his shirt, loose woollen pants with buckskin sewn over the seat and along the inner thighs.

Like Lamar and Keogh, Hart wore one pistol strapped to his hip. In his case the holster held a Colt Peacemaker .45 with a mother-of-pearl grip on which was carved a Mexican emblem showing an eagle with a snake gripped between its claws and in its beak.

So that the holster would angle correctly in a sitting position, Hart had loosened the tie-string which normally fastened inside his thigh. The safety thong was still in place over the curved hammer.

Out of sight and inside his right boot, he had a well-honed double-bladed Apache knife.

Charlie Webb leaned back against his desk and ostentatiously lit a long cigar. He drew and puffed, puffed and drew and finally tossed the spent match into the corner of the room, where it joined a number of others, a mound of dust and a couple of dead spiders. The Texas Rangers had been in Webb's office for the best part of half an hour and all they had heard so far was the deputy's boasting about what he was going to do with Mannen Clements and John Wesley Hardin when he got them in his gun sights.

Marvin Peake, who rode with Webb and also with the late

Jack Helm, leaned his weight against the back wall and smirked while Webb performed.

If he was amused and entertained, the Rangers were not. Lefty O'Neal less than the rest. He sat there, looking less than comfortable even before Webb had begun, sucking his moustache down into his mouth and kicking his heels into the floorboards at the same time as he cracked his knuckles and grimaced openly.

Eventually, Webb could ignore Lefty no longer.

'Somethin' crawlin' up your skin?' asked Webb, the cigar wobbling up and down at the corner of his mouth.

Lefty unwound his legs and stretched them out in front of him; they stretched an awful long way. He nodded slowly and looked into Webb's face. 'Yeah', he said just as slowly. 'Yeah, it is.'

'Then maybe you'd best spit it off your chest and say what it is.'

Lefty hung back his head, hawked up some phlegm noisily, swirled it around inside his mouth and jerked his head forward. A flob of yellow spittle landed on the floor no more than a foot in front of Charlie Webb and splashed against his boots.

Webb chomped down on his cigar; his eyes bulged and his hand started to move towards his gun.

Lefty didn't bat an eyelid; he didn't need to. Three hands covered the butts of three guns and three thumbs began to lever three hammers back. Charlie Webb's fingers had still to touch the polished wooden grip of his .44.

Peake stared on, his mouth dropping open slowly. Surely they weren't going to gun the sheriff down in his own office?

Seconds ticked by.

They were not.

Charlie Webb glanced nervously around the room, for those moments shaken from the arrogant self-assurance which usually shielded him from anything and everyone. Then it passed. He nodded his head generously, moved his hand ostentatiously away from his holster and towards the cigar in his mouth, withdrew the cigar and chuckled.

'Damn thing's gone out on me.'

He pulled a match from his vest pocket and struck it against the corner of the desk.

'About this Hardin business,' said Lefty easily, yet staring hard at Webb all the same, 'maybe we'd best hear what happened down in Albuquerque.'

Webb drew on his cigar, threw the match into the corner and grinned. 'Marv here, he was in Albuquerque at the time. He can tell it best.'

Marvin Peake scratched the side of his hatchet face nervously as the eyes of the Rangers turned to scrutinize him. His tongue flicked, lizard-like, over the dry skin of his chapped lips and his hooded eyes blinked furiously.

Charlie Webb pulled a medicine bottle of brandy from one of the drawers of his desk and tossed it over to Peake, who juggled it against his chest before bringing it under control. 'Take a pull on that first.'

Marvin gulped a couple of swallows down and would have taken a third, had Webb's hand not been already stretched out towards him. Before he could begin his tale, the bottle was back out of sight.

'I was in Albuquerque along of Jack Helm and four or five others. Things were pretty hot down there an' we was all jumpy as hell. Just a couple of days before two of the boys had ridden into a bunch of Taylor's men out on the plain. They hightailed it out of there fast as they could an' they was lucky to get away from 'em without stoppin' a bullet.'

Webb leaned forward from where he was now sitting on the desk top. 'Few months before this happened, there'd been a shootin' over in Cuero and that sure upped the temperature some. Hardin and a few others were in town settin' up a cattle sale and they had a few drinks to help 'em on their way. Seems one of Jack's deputies had been helping himself to a few whiskies too many and he took it into his head to give Hardin a piece of his mind.'

Charlie Webb grinned at the Rangers and gave his cigar a deep draw before continuing.

'This deputy, Morgan his name was, he weren't satisfied

leavin' it at words. He swaggers out into the street after Hardin and the other Taylor boys and tells Hardin he's puttin' him under arrest.' Webb laughed brokenly. 'Goes for his gun. Way I heard the rest of it, young Hardin he lets Morgan get the damn thing all but clear an' then he pulls his own pistol and whops two slugs into Morgan's chest. Morgan went down like he'd been back-kicked by a brace of mules, not quite dead an' hollerin' for help. Hardin goes over to him, calm as you please, sets the pistol barrel close to Morgan's head and gives him all the help he needs.'

Webb waited a few moments, enjoying the attention. His broad face broke into a smile and he gestured with his cigar, pantomiming Hardin's actions.

'Yes, sir, blasted ole J.B. Morgan's head across the boardwalk and half-way up the wall of the general store.' He pointed a finger towards the centre of the room. 'Dumb bastard!' he said.

Lefty O'Neal pulled at one side of his moustache and suggested it would be a good idea to get back to what happened in Albuquerque. Marvin Peake glanced at Webb for permission to continue, wet his dry lips and carried on.

'Like I said, like Charlie just explained, we was all jumpy as cats on heat, knowin' that there could be a bloody battle any moment, any place. Even there in town. Well, we was headin' down past the livery stable when someone, I can't recall who it was exactly, but he says, ain't they a couple of Taylor's horse out front of the smithy? Jack, he quietens us down and steps over and takes a look and sure enough, it's the right brand.

'I don't mind tellin' you, I reckoned we stood with pretty good odds, bein' six-handed an' all and there only bein' two of them. Course ...' Peake rubbed at the side of his nose and wriggled his head a little, '... we wasn't to know which two. Not right off anyway. Jack, he sends one of the boys over to take a closer look and when he comes back we can see from the expression on his face it's one of the big ones, Clements maybe, or Hardin, even Taylor hisself.

'Course, it turned out to be Jim Taylor and Wes Hardin.'

Peake rubbed his nose again as if it was irritating him something dreadful. 'That kind of changed the odds somethin', accordin' to my lights, but Jack Helm, he must've still reckoned we had 'em cold. He ordered one of us to untie the two mounts and lead 'em quietly up the street, Hardin an' Taylor they're inside talkin' with the smithy and such. Maybe one of their horses is goin' to need a shoe and sure enough when they pulled away, one of 'em's got a limp at the front. They hear what's goin' on from inside and hurry out, the blacksmith close behind 'em. Soon as they hit the boards they're smack into us. Half a dozen of us and all armed up like we was meanin' business.

'Hardin and Taylor they exchange glances and see their mounts've been moved up the street. Right then I thought we'd got 'em. Neither of those boys looked like they was about to make a fight of it. Jack, he must've thought so, too. He steps up towards 'em and his pistol's already out of his holster and coverin' the two of 'em.

'"John Wesley Hardin," he says, clear as day, "I'm arrestin' you for the murder of Deputy J. B. Morgan in Cuero, April last." Nobody moves for a minute, then Hardin he turns his head to Taylor an' says, "Looks like the game is up, Jim. He's got me to rights." Taylor made some remark, I don't know what. Jack motions with his gun for Hardin to step off the boardwalk so's he could put the cuffs on him. He don't move awful fast so Jack told Hamie Miller to get in there and shift him down. Hamie's got a sawn-off tucked into his side and he looks like he'd use it if'n he had to. Hardin seems to reckon this, too, on account of he widens his eyes when Hamie closes on him and nods and says okay an' steps down towards him.'

Peake's voice snagged in his throat and he coughed and snaked his tongue over his mouth.

'Next thing I see, Jim Taylor makes some move towards the smith an' Jack's pistol swings round to cover him. Right about then, Hardin must've jumped Hamie. Anyways, Hamie's staggerin' back with blood comin' from a busted nose an' Hardin's got the shotgun. Jack screams at him and tries to get a shot in but all Hardin does is pump both barrels into him from about fifteen feet.

'Jack, he hits the ground like a sack of grain 'cept that he's losing blood all over. Everyone's shoutin' and yellin' but there's no one doin' much. Taylor he jerks a pistol from his belt an' next thing I see he's firin' it into Jack Helm's head.'

Peake paused to wipe a fine spray of spittle away from his chin; every eye in the room was on him.

' I see him layin' there an' twitchin', his hand an' arm leapin' clear off the ground, fingers curlin' an' all.' Peake glanced quickly at Webb. 'His head was half blown away. That didn't seem to stop his hand . . .'

Peake faltered to a halt and Webb sighed and produced the bottle of brandy. Fortified, the man continued in a lower voice.

'Hardin, he throwed the shotgun down and pulled his own pistol, him an' Taylor they told us to back off while Hardin he ordered the blacksmith to fetch his mount and get on with changin' his busted shoe.'

'Five of you,' Lefty O'Neal interrupted.

'Huh?'

'I said, there was five of you left alive.'

'Yeah, I guess, yeah, that's right, five.'

'Two of them.'

'Yeah, only.'

'Only what?'

We'd seen what they'd done to Jack. Shot him in cold blood like that. They weren't goin' to bother none about droppin' any one of us. Not after they'd killed a peace officer right there in the street.'

'And the rest of the town?' asked Lefty.

'Hell, they'd locked up their doors and shutteıed their windows and that was all they wanted to know.

Lefty shook his head, unwound his long legs and stretched them out before him. Peake waited to make sure the Ranger wasn't about to ask any more questions.

'Get on with it,' said Webb impatiently. 'Or have you finished this particular tale of glory?'

Marv Peake shrugged self-consciously. 'They kept us there at gunpoint while that shoe was fixed. Jack bleedin' into the street all the time. Flies buzzin' round him an' such. One of the fellers, he asks Hardin if he can drag the body off but Hardin he just laughed and said he didn't care if Jack Helm stayed there till he rot.' Peake glanced at Webb once more. 'Soon as the horse was shod, they rode out.'

'An' you got up a posse and chased after 'em?' asked Lefty bitterly.

Peake didn't answer. Not in words. The hangdog expression and the refusal to meet the Ranger's eyes were answer enough.

There was silence in the room for some moments. Charlie Webb trying to think of something to say but words, for once, failing him. It was left to O'Neal to push his long frame up from the chair and look at the deputy sherriff and say: 'You got some fine lawmen in these parts, I'll say that for you.'

'Meaning what?' asked Webb, anger burring his voice. He knew only too well what the Ranger meant.

'Meaning one man who's foolhardy enough to go up against a couple of gunslingers without givin' it a second's thought, and five others who ain't got the balls of a one-year-old bullock.'

He looked quickly at Peake to see if the man would react, but Peake was as unlikely to take on Lefty as he had been John Wesley Hardin.

Charlie Webb took a pace towards O'Neal, determined to show that he was unafraid. 'What Jack Helm did was a brave act. Jack was a brave man and he deserved better than getting killed the way he did. Hardin and Taylor proved what sort of cowardly killers they are and I'll tell you this, Mister Texas Ranger, I'll tell all of you men, the next time either of those murderers show their face round me, they'll be the ones who get flattened in the street and don't get back up till someone picks 'em up and throws 'em to the dogs.' He jabbed a finger at the tall man's chest. 'You remember Charlie Webb said that. And what Charlie Webb says ain't nobody goin' to make a lie out of.'

Lefty O'Neal held Webb's gaze for just long enough to let

the man know that he thought he was talking through his ass. Then, without a word, he turned and led the other Rangers out of the lawman's office.

'All piss an' vinegar, ain't he?' said Lamar as soon as they were outside.

Keogh chuckled good-humouredly. 'Yeah, an' I always thought you had everyone else beat when it come to braggin' 'bout what you done and what you're goin' to do.'

Lamar whipped off his stetson and flapped it hard towards Keogh's face, the Ranger shielding himself with his arm and still laughing.

'Cut it out, you two,' said O'Neal, gripping the pommel of his saddle and hauling himself up. 'You'll likely get all the fightin' you can handle where you're headin'.'

Both men stopped, stared at him. 'Where's that?' Keogh asked.

'Albuquerque.'

'What in God's name for?' asked Lamar.

O'Neal shrugged and half-grinned. 'Look around. Careful, though. More than half the folk down there think Hardin's some kind of hero for gettin' rid of Helm the way he did. You watch you don't get backshot, that's all.'

'How 'bout you an' Wes?' asked Keogh.

'Hardin's got a place of his own. Young wife. We'll drop down that way and pay a social call.'

'Make good apple pie, does she?' grinned Lamar.

Lefty O'Neal laughed. 'Maybe we'll find out.'

'Yeah, maybe you will.'

When all four men were mounted up, they rode down the main street side by side, dividing into pairs beyond the town limits, briefly acknowledging each other with a wave before pulling their mounts in different directions. Back in his office, Charlie Webb swallowed hard at the brandy and cursed them to all hell. If they met up with John Wesley Hardin, he hoped the young gunman gave them the same treatment as he'd meted out to Jack Helm. Webb didn't want no Ranger taking Hardin in – that was something he'd reserved for himself.

Five

Wes Hart had responded to the news that the Texas Rangers were reforming with little enough apparent thought. Back in Texas for no more than six months after a spell scouting for the army against the Navajo, Hart had grafted a few dollars here and there without really settling. It had been his second time with the military – the second since the end of the War Between the States – and there had been little enough about it to enjoy. Most of his trouble had been caused by an officer called Rodway, whose understanding of the Indians was matched only by his humanity and common sense. As far as Rodway was concerned the soldier's Bible was his army manual and what that taught him about respecting the Indians' way of life could be written with one finger in a very small patch of sand. So for months, Hart had done his best to hold off Rodway's most martinet excesses and had succeeded in making a genuine friend amongst the Navajo. The chief's wearing blanket that he always carried with him in his saddle bag was a testimony to that. Woven from hand-spun blue, red and white wool yarns, it was striped with a row of irregular star-shaped patterns at the edges and centre. Like the Apache knife he kept in his boot, the blanket was more than a souvenir: it was a constant reminder of the bravery of a civilization that was in the process of being broken up by a larger, greedier white one. A white civilization that had spawned men like Charlie Webb, like John Wesley Hardin.

It had also spawned himself – Wes Hart did not think of that. Not then.

He thought about his decision to join the Rangers and so far he figured there was little enough to regret about it. He had met some good men – some fools, too, but they were everywhere – and there was a comradeship that recalled some of his times riding with Colonel John R. Baylor's Confederate Volunteers. That had been in the early days of the war when everything seemed possible, even victory. It had been before the progressive use of infantry ordnance had resulted in men on both sides being shelled to death or permanent injury by their own side; before the dreadful wasting diseases had swept through both armies, finally killing more than bullet and bayonet and shell put together.

Certainly it was better than the job Hart had been holding down when he heard that the Rangers were recruiting again. After a month or so driving freight wagons across the north of the state, he had signed on with the Circle B ranch as a cowboy, busting his butt all day long and in all weathers for hot chow, a crowded bunkhouse and scarcely enough money to buy a glass of whisky on the rare visits to town. He had announced his intention of quitting to the foreman with a sense of some great weight being raised from his shoulders. When the foreman heard what Hart intended to do, he called him for a fool, volunteering to take not much more money in exchange for the chance of getting shot at like he was the prize at a turkey shoot.

Hart had shrugged and collected his gear from the bunkhouse, saddling up his mount and riding the couple of hundred miles that took him to his first interview with Captain Armstrong. By the time that session was over, Hart was as good as certain that his instincts had been right and the Circle B foreman had been wrong. When he was set to ride with Lefty O'Neal a couple of weeks later, his mind was made up.

'You know you got the same damn name,' said Lefty out of the blue, their horses trotting along the ill-formed dirt road.

'Huh?'

'Same name. More or less. You and Hardin.'

'Wesley, you mean?'

'Sure, Wesley. That is your name, ain't it? I mean, what Wes is short for?'

Hart nodded: 'I guess.'

'You don't know?'

'I know.'

'It's Wesley, then?'

'Yeah.'

'Strange, ain't it. The name bein' the same.'

Hart didn't give it a deal of thought. 'No,' he said.

Lefty shrugged his shoulders and gave the reins a little flick. A mile or so later, he leaned over in the saddle and said, 'He was English, you know?'

Hart just looked at him.

'Wesley.'

'Oh yeah?'

'John Wesley. Lived back in the last century. Started a whole new religion, more or less.'

'What of it?'

'That's where the name comes from.'

'Whose damned name?'

'Wesley.'

Hart shook his head. 'Not mine, it don't.'

'Uh-uh. His. Hardin's. John Wesley Hardin. That's for John Wesley. His father bein' a preacher. Methodist. That's the religion this first John Wesley started up.'

'What's so all-fired different about it?'

'Methodism?'

'Yeah.'

Lefty considered the question for a few hundred yards. He was skinned if he knew the answer and he said so.

'They still use the book, don't they?' asked Hart.

'The book?'

'The Bible.'

'I guess so.'

Hart grinned. 'Maybe that makes us Methodists, too.' He reached back and patted one of his saddle bags. When a man joined the Texas Rangers he was presented with two Bibles; one was the real thing and the other contained a list of wanted men whose duty it was for the Rangers to bring to justice.

Neither man said anything further until Lefty signalled they should turn off the road towards a small creek that was running down from the foothills to the north-east and give their horses a breather. When the saddle cinches were loosened and the animals had drunk their fill and were grazing patches of coarse grass and clumps of shrub, Lefty drew out a metal flask and offered it to Hart.

'Ain't just Charlie Webb as keeps a supply,' he grinned, easing his long frame down to the hard ground.

'Thanks.' Hart took a pull from the flask and handed it back, squatting down close and pulling the makings of a cigarette from his vest pockets. He rolled two, one for Lefty and one for himself. When both were lit and drawing well, Lefty leaned on one long arm and said, 'Funny, ain't it. Young feller with a preacher for a father, turning out wild the way Hardin's done.'

Hart thought about it, shrugged, the thin cigarette cupped in the fingers of his right hand. 'Sometimes I heard it can turn a boy the other way, overmuch prayin' and suchlike. Send him real wild.'

Lefty's eyebrows were raised. 'Looks like that's what happened with Hardin. Though that don't seem reason enough.' He pursed his lips together and let a smoke ring drift upwards, catching on the breeze and dispersing until no trace could be seen. 'Maybe you don't need a reason. Maybe some are born that way and what their folk do, the way they're brung up, that don't have a mess to do with it.'

Hart was thinking about the war and the way that had changed folk, not the ones it maimed or blinded or whose land it burnt, but the ones it changed in other ways, changed inside. He thought about reconstruction and the way in which that seemed to be dragging much of Texas into two opposing factions, of which the Sutton–Taylor feud was but one small, vicious part. He thought these things and half of him wanted to speak them out loud, while the rest of him didn't want to get involved, couldn't be bothered, the time for talking about them might come but it wasn't now.

'What you thinkin'?' asked Lefty.

Hart shook his head. 'Nothin',' he said.

The next time they stopped Lefty asked him about his own folks, about his own father and if he wasn't some kind of preacher or at least keen on religion that he should name his son after a famous Englishman who spent most of his life stumping around the land giving sermons and thumping the good book.

Hart didn't want to talk about that either. Not a great deal. But Lefty wasn't about to let it alone that easy. Finally, Hart reckoned it was easier to talk than stay silent.

'Tell the truth,' he said, 'I don't remember him at all. Not really. I wasn't but three when he died and I guess I was a couple of years older than that before I figured out what that meant. I always figured I must've seen it as somethin' like goin' into town to the store, only a longer trip on account of the time it took him to come back with the candy and liquorice. Two long, cold winters before I got it into my head there weren't goin' to be no liquorice. Not from him, anyway.'

'You got no picture of him?' asked Lefty, leaning forward. 'No memory back of your head some place?'

Hart wasted the remainder of his cigarette between his fingers. 'There's somethin' there, but it ain't clear. Never was. More like a shape off to one side, bendin' down. Down to me, I guess. Could be to hand me that damn twist of black liquorice, I don't know. But that's all there is, this dark . . .' Hart gestured vainly with his hands, as if that might help him to find the word, '. . . thing somewhere there at the corner of my eye, only when I turn towards it, it's gone.'

Lefty breathed out lightly, smoke drifting up from the centre of his long, drooping moustache. 'What happened?' he asked in a flat voice.

'He was fightin' for the Californias. Wanted to keep California independent from the Union.'

'Like a Civil War before the Civil War,' put in Lefty.

Hart nodded. 'Somethin' like. Anyhow, I never knew for certain what happened and if my ma did she never told me. We just rode out there one day in the wagon, that was when I was five, that was when I knew, knew for certain, and she showed me this plot of raised ground and the marker. Writin' on it she said was my father's name, only I couldn't make no sense of it. But that was where he lay and he weren't travellin' anywhere else. No candy. No liquorice.'

Lefty grunted into the silence that followed and made as if to stand up and move on, but now that Hart had begun there were other things on his mind that needed saying.

'Same year she took me out to my father's grave, same day, we went on out to this place Folsom way. Right in the foothills of the Sierras. Some shack there with tumble-down rockers for siftin' gold from the dirt that rolled down stream and all of a sudden my ma was pointin' out this feller to me, whiskers and a battered old bowler hat, and sayin' this is your new pa.

'I can remember that clear enough. Standin' there like the fool kid I was just lookin' up at him, not understandin'. Ma tryin' to fix some kind of smile on her face that would mean it was goin' to be all right, though when I thought back about it later, I could see that she weren't certain at all. This feller he says things to me that I didn't hear and then he grabs me and I struggle and kick on account of I'm sure he's goin' to wallop me one. He laughs and my ma, she gets all worried and shouts for me to calm down, and then this big whiskery face comes in real close and kisses me and amongst all the sweat and dirt I can smell the drink already.'

Hart stretched his head backwards until all he could see was the flat blue of the sky. He stared at it for several moments, aware that Lefty was tending to the mounts, making them ready to travel on.

'You okay?' Lefty said after a few minutes.

Hart brought down his head and nodded, got up fast and smooth and took his reins from Lefty's hand.

'Let's ride,' Hart said, slotting his boot into the stirrup. 'Let's get the hell out of here.'

The Hardin place was a long, flat-roofed building with a low fence out front which was supposed to give some protection to the vegetable garden that someone was struggling to breathe life into. The doors and windows had had their frames painted recently, a bright green colour that contrasted oddly with the grey-brown shades of the planking and split logs from which the place was made. One of the windows sported glass and back of it two narrow strips of red curtain material hung down. The other windows were tacked over with loose sacking. Smoke drifted through the lopsided tin chimney at the centre of the roof.

Off to the side someone was half-way through building a lean-to, the frame set firmly in place and one wall almost there. A couple of mares were coralled at the back and close by there was a hen house with a rooster flapping his wings from the nearest arch. A few chickens pecked absent-mindedly at the dirt and ignored him for now.

Lefty and Hart exchanged glances and Hart loosed the rifle in its bucket holster to the left of his saddle.

A face appeared between the strips of red curtain and peered out. They heard a bolt being slammed shut on the far side of the door.

'What d'you reckon?' asked Lefty.

Hart shook his head. 'I reckon he ain't here.'

Lefty motioned for Hart to stay where he was and walked his horse round the property, taking his time and keeping his hand close by the gun at his belt. The rooster crowed up a storm like Lefty was somehow challenging him for his territory. It was the only thing that happened.

'Anythin'?' asked Hart when the other Ranger got back.

'Nothin'.'

'You want to wait around? Ride out? What?'

'I ain't sure.'

Hart looked at the house, glanced at the neatly spaced pieces of stick that were holding up nothing much in the garden. 'I think we should talk with her,' he said.

Lefty nodded. 'Okay.'

'Best cover me,' said Hart and climbed down.

He was but three paces inside the fence when the dark grey barrel of a rifle poked underneath the sacking of one of the windows. Hart looked directly at it and raised both hands so that they were level with his shoulders, but spread out before him. He kept on walking. Back of him, he heard the triple click of Lefty's Colt hammer locking back.

The rifle barrel poked out a little further; it was almost steady.

'You don't come no further!'

Hart took precisely two more paces and stopped. The rifle was fixed to hit him right about the breast bone, allowing for an upward jerk when it recoiled.

'You say your piece from there.'

'Mrs Hardin?'

No answer: no movement.

'Mrs Hardin, ma'am . . .'

From inside, the sound of a child suddenly waking, beginning to cry.

'Mrs Hardin, I'm Wes Hart. Me and my partner, we're Texas Rangers. We'd like to talk to your husband if he's home.'

The noise of the child rose to a keen edge. The rifle wavered.

'Ma'am . . .'

Hart took another step forward and the woman shouted for him to stop.

He stopped; the child didn't. The rooster set up in competition.

'Ma'am, if we could talk . . .'

'You know my husband ain't here.'

'Yes, ma'am, but if we could . . .'

'Ride back where you come from and leave us alone!' Anger made her voice shake but she kept the rifle steady. Almost still. Anger and maybe the beginning of tears. The child was screaming.

'Mrs Hardin, if you want to tend to the child I give you my word I won't come any closer'n I am now.'

'Your word!' she spat back at him.

'Yes, ma'am.'

He knew that she was staring at him through a narrow slit in the sacking, trying to make up her mind whether she could believe him, wanting to, wanting to comfort her baby.

Hart kept his hands spread, fingers just separated. The child's screams dipped down and he thought for a moment that she was going to lay quiet, but right off they rose up again, lustier than ever. The rifle barrel pulled quickly back through the sacking and almost at once the sounds of shouting caught and stammered and then were all but gone.

Hart lowered his hands to his side but otherwise he made no movement.

The bolt back of the door was slid back.

She was smaller than Hart imagined, the woman who had been called Jane Bowen. No more than medium height at best and slender, with her hair cut short and dark so that she might pass for a boy. The child in her arms was perhaps a year old, already obviously a girl. Fairer hair than her mother and curly, long enough to suggest that as she grew so it would wind down at her back. For an instant Hart considered how the woman might look like that, her hair long, dark, curled down her back. The way it had been, perhaps, when she and John Wesley Hardin had stood side by side, the one hand over the other and the preacher's words . . .

'What is it you want?'

Her eyes, dark, flicked past Hart to the tall, moustached man in the saddle then back to Hart again.

'Your husband . . .'

'I told you he ain't here.'

'I know, ma'am. But that was why we rode out an' . . .'

'And now you know he isn't here?'

'I figured, if we spoke with you . . .'

'You'd what?'

Hart wiped his forefinger and thumb down either side of his mouth. The little girl stirred and snuggled against her mother's almost flat bosom.

'You know where your husband is, ma'am?'

'Of course I do.'

'And . . .'

'And it's none of your business.'

'We wanted to talk with him 'bout a shootin' in Albuquerque.'

Her dark eyes flickered, all but smiled.

'A peace officer was shot,' said Lefty from back of the fence.

The eyes changed and she laughed but there was no humour in it. 'A peace officer! Is that what you call him? Jack Helm was a drunken braggart who took his pay out of Sutton's pockets. Is that what you call peace officer?' She looked at Lefty, then at Hart. 'Is that the kind of peace officers you are?'

'We don't take nothin' from Sutton,' said Lefty smarting. 'Not him nor anyone else.'

'Then you're the first lawman I ever heard of as didn't,' she snapped back.

'In that case, ma'am,' said Lefty, 'we're the first Texas Rangers you ever met.'

She looked at him darkly and made as if to turn away and go back inside the house. One of the hens was pecking at something trying to grow in the garden and she clucked at it and shooed it off. The little girl began to whimper and she cuddled her down, one hand behind her head.

'You know what happened in Albuquerque?' asked Hart.

She looked at him side-on. 'I know my husband was there with Jim Taylor arranging to sell some stock and that Jack Helm came up on them with half a dozen men and tried to force John into a fight.'

'He didn't have a lot of trouble doin' that,' put in Lefty.

The woman ignored him and continued to speak to Hart. 'Helm set one of his men at John's back with a shotgun and tried to take his weapon from him. That's what I know.'

'Maybe he figured it was his duty to arrest your husband,' Hart suggested.

'Arrest him?'

'On account of a couple of months before that he'd shot another lawman named Morgan.'

'Another drunk!'

'Killin's killin',' Hart protested.

'And what do you think would have happened there in Albuquerque if John had given Jack Helm his gun? With a shotgun already on his back.' Her eyes fixed Hart firmly.

'Don't you think there'd have been killin' there?'

Hart sucked in his bottom lip. There wasn't any answer he could make and both of them knew it.

'There's more folk in these parts think John's a hero for doin' what he done than reckon it was any wrong.'

'That's as maybe.'

'It's more'n that. What matters? What folk think or what some bought-an'-paid-for lawman takes it into his head to do?'

The child started to fidget and the occasional cry came from her mouth as her small fists hit her mother's chest. Jane Hardin looked hard into Hart's face and turned fully away. Hart watched her go, hair cut short above the nape of the neck, suggestion of curve and dip as her back slendered down. The bolt slammed back fast. Hart kicked at the ground and swung back towards his horse. Neither man spoke for a long time, till the Hardin place was almost out of sight.

Six

Not above two weeks later Hart and Lefty O'Neal rode into Paradise Spring on Rangers business. There'd been complaints for some time that a lot of the rustling that had been going on in the area had been centring on that small community, half-hidden in the lee of the Montero foothills. A certain amount of stock loss was accepted by most of the big cattlemen – after all, how else had they got started themselves? – but numbers in this part of the state were increasing and it wasn't any longer a business to ignore. What with the Sutton–Taylor affair going on all around and more and more likely to break out into unaccountable violence, those cattle ranchers who were doing their best to keep clear of trouble and still make a more than tidy profit figured that someone owed them a little protection.

With most of the state police and the county sheriffs either in Sutton's pockets or just not anxious to get involved, the cattlemen turned to the Rangers.

While you're down there checking Hardin out, take a look at Paradise Spring and keep a few of these people quiet. Get them off my back for a while. Those had been Captain Armstrong's words, more or less. And so the two Texas Rangers had made a forty or fifty mile loop away from the Hardin place and headed for Paradise.

When they got there, it sure didn't look like Paradise was supposed to.

For a start there was a noticeable lack of angels, and the heavenly voices and harps had somehow become the whining of a mongrel mutt that was chained up out front of the general store and the tuneless singing of an old timer who seemed content to sit in the middle of the street, plucking threads from the cuffs of his worn-out coat and the bottoms of his shiny black pants. If he sat there long enough he'd be down to a pair of stained and darned long johns.

Hart and Lefty separated, swinging their mounts around the old man, who carried on with his task as if they weren't there.

Whoever had been responsible for building one side of the street – no more than a dozen and a half structures with flat roofs and bowed and warped walls – hadn't been inspired to get on with the other half. Apart from a couple of heavy-duty tarpaulin tents and what looked to be a dog kennel, there was nothing there to prevent the wind hammering straight off the hills and whipping the dirt up on to the forty yards of narrow boardwalk and covering it over.

Back of the buildings, the sails of a wind pump turned lazily now, no more than a breeze in the humid air. Both men were sticky with sweat and too much trail dust and their throats were dry as snakeskin.

'So this is Paradise?' said Lefty mockingly.

Hart half-turned in the saddle, running his eyes along the store, a saddlers', a boarded-up dining rooms, the barber shop with its solitary chair filled by the barber himself, aproned and reading an already yellowing newspaper, another boarded-up building, this one formerly a bank, a saloon, the livery stable and another store.

'Maybe for some folk,' he said.

'If there's rustlers holed up here they sure ain't makin' a lot of money.'

Hart patted his horse's neck, the animal hot beneath his hand. 'You want to look around?'

'We're here. We'd best do something. Aside from gettin' a couple of drinks, that is.'

Hart glanced over at the saloon. 'You want to do that first?'

'Maybe we should see to the horses.'

Hart nodded. 'Okay. You want to take 'em or shall I?'

'I'll see to it. Why don't you get us a couple of beers set up. That is, if they got beer in this one-eyed place.' He laughed. 'Jesus! I knew it weren't right they could have no cattle thieves in Paradise.'

Hart swung down from the saddle, grinning. He handed his reins up to his partner and said, 'See they get a good rub-down an' some feed. I don't guess we'll be stickin' round here too long.'

'Okay.'

The mongrel stopped whining and barked instead, jagged, broken sounds like each one was tearing at his throat. The old timer had got bored with taking his clothes to pieces and was lying flat on his back with both legs lifted up in the air and his arms spread out sideways.

'Damn!' said Hart quietly, scratching the back of his head under the brim of his flat-crowned hat. 'Damn!'

He was half-way to the saloon when Lefty called over his shoulder: 'Don't drink my beer before your own.'

Hart raised his left hand in acknowledgment and stepped up on to the sidewalk. Most of the boards were cracked or cracking, the gaps between them silted up. He could smell the rancid stink of tallow burning inside the saloon before he pushed open the door. One lamp swung lightly from a hook in the centre of the ceiling, the other smouldered at the far end of the bar, which was no more than several lengths of wood resting on four barrels close by the rear wall. Along from the right-hand barrels there was a back door.

In the smoky half-dark – there were no windows and the only light came in above and below the doors – Hart saw a huddle of men around one of the tables playing dominoes. At another table four men had their heads bent over a poker game. A couple of others sat idly talking over an almost empty bottle. A woman with fair curly hair and a smudged red mouth was playing patience at a table set away from the rest. She glanced up at Hart as he came in, took in the gun-belt and holster, the set of his body; she decided he was handsome enough but that whatever money he had in his pockets was unlikely to come her way. She shrugged and set the four of hearts down on the five of spades.

The men surveyed Hart too, the way men did in a place where strangers were few and far between. They were still looking at him as he walked across towards the bar.

One of the domino players grated his chair back and followed him to the back of the room.

'Yeah?' he asked, feet shuffling in broken-backed shoes.

Hart waited until the man was behind the long table, taking the opportunity to give the place the once-over. He couldn't see all the faces clearly, but those he did failed to strike any chords.

'You got beer?' he asked.

'Sure we got beer. What kind of . . .?'

'Two,' said Hart. 'Two beers.'

The man cocked his head to one side, gave Hart an extra-careful look and said, 'Thirsty, huh? Rid a long way?' He tried not to make the sideways glance towards the rear door too obvious, but it would have been like hiding a bull among a herd of cows on heat.

Hart angled his body round to cover whoever the barkeep was expecting. 'Sure,' he said, not bothering to explain, 'that's it, thirsty.'

The barman managed not to look too apprehensive while wiping the dust out of a couple of glasses. Over by the side wall the woman cursed quietly; she had five cards left and the only way she could get them out was to cheat.

'Hey! Hey, there! Anyone around?'

The man who limped forward was no more than half Lefty O'Neal's height and less than half his weight. His skinny arm rested on a stick which he hopped along beside the useless swing of a skinny leg.

'You in charge here?'

The man's head gave a nervous shake and his right eye blinked down.

'Work here?'

'Just . . . just lookin' after the place for a while . . . McCann, he's out of town right now . . . said would I . . .' The sentence petered out to nothing.

Lefty looked round the stalls, four of them holding horses. Bales of straw. Buckets. Curry combs and brushes. Three long-handled rakes strangely neat side-by-side on the wall. A wilderness of hay was piled high against the half-wall at the rear. Beyond that Lefty could see the fencing of a corral and some more horses penned inside.

'Like to leave these,' he said.

The man looked uneasy, uncertain.

'You ain't goin' to turn away business, are you?'

'I ain't sure.' The man hesitated.

'Just a brush-down, some oats an' water.'

The man glanced at his stock, at the useless leg. 'I ain't sure . . .'

'You can pay some kid to work 'em down, can't you?'

The right eye blinked again but at least he seemed to have stopped arguing.

'Fine,' said Lefty. 'How much?'

'I . . .'

'Don't tell me you ain't sure.' Lefty started to back away. 'I'll settle up when we come back. An' don't worry 'bout gettin' paid. Them are Rangers' mounts an' they'll get paid for fair an' square.'

A smile on his face, Lefty turned away. If he heard the first movement behind him, he heard it too late, reacted too slow. From the corner of his left eye he glimpsed a man rising up from the hay like a swimmer bursting upwards through water. A black patch strapped across his face, covering his right eye. Bald, uncovered head. A largely toothless grin. Winchester rifle angled up from his side, the stock pulled against his hip. It fired twice. Lefty felt the kick, the lurching hammer that drove into his ribs, his chest; he staggered sideways. Always away, always trying to turn. Lengths of straw, wisps of hay seemed to be falling slowly from the bald head. Slowly.

Lefty crashed into the floor and grunted with pain. He tried to roll on to his back, freeing his arm. Tried, but ... there were three men now. Pistols. Still the patch and the toothless grin, but another with grey hair, a third who was little more than a kid, freckles spread across his nose like ... like ...

Lefty knew he had to pull his guns free from the holsters. Both. Either. The crack and blurt of gunfire filled the high barn, echoing shrilly. The old timer flattened himself against the nearest wall, his body shaking. Not wanting to see the way the Ranger bucked and arched awkwardly into the air as the bullets ripped through him.

Lefty managed to lift his right-hand gun. Pain screamed from his left leg and he saw what looked like his knee cap hanging through a gap in his pants. Horses kicked inside their stalls. Others were ready, saddled, at the rear. Men running. Lefty tried once more to lift his arm, bring the gun level but his muscles refused to obey. He lurched suddenly forwards and there was nothing he could do to prevent the side of his face smacking hard against the ground.

For moments his consciousness toyed with him, jerking him in and out of blackness. Hoofbeats seemed to gallop over him and he tried to huddle beneath the crook of one arm. His mouth and nostrils filled with blood and his eyes ... how could his eyes be full of blood?

Hart – where was Hart?

Lefty opened his mouth to call out and choked on blood and vomit.

He couldn't be dying. Not there, like that, suddenly and for no reason that he understood. One moment a man rising up out of the straw and then . . .

West Hart had one of the glasses of beer to his mouth when the first shots sounded down the street. Two and close together. Rifle shots? He banged the glass down hard, already moving away. Between himself and the door, the two talkers stumbled their hands towards what little remained in their bottle. Dominoes clattered to the ground. The rear door scraped and Hart stopped in mid-stride and swung round, hand moving automatically towards the Colt .45 at his side. Two of the poker players were getting to their feet and at least one of them was fanning his hand out over his holster. Hart shouted a warning and the movement stopped. The door kept on opening.

Hart watched it, Colt in hand.

He watched the wrong door.

The man who came through from the back was sixty years old, hunch-backed and already three-parts drunk. John Wesley Hardin had paid him to go round that way – the price of a shot of whisky. Himself, he used the front.

Hart spun round fast. He all but recognized Hardin right off from the likenesses on the fliers, but he wasn't sure. That didn't matter. What did was a man with a pistol tight in his fist and an expression on his handsome face that said, I can use this.

The two men faced one another, weapons aimed forward and hammers cocked. A fractional move of either index finger and at that range it was likely to be fatal.

'I smelt law,' said Hardin.

Hart spread his left hand a little, said nothing.

'You with Sutton, like all the rest?'

'Texas Ranger,' said Hart flatly.

A volley of gunfire sounded from up the street and Hart made as if to move towards the door but a slight shrug of Hardin's gun stopped him.

'How come Paradise is so honoured?' Hardin asked.

'Cattle rustlers,' said Hart shortly, looking beyond Hardin towards the street.

'Not lookin' for me, I suppose?'

Hart's eyes narrowed. 'That depends who you are.'

'John Wesley Hardin.'

'Wes Hart.'

Hardin's handsome mouth twitched and Hart thought he was going to fire. 'I told Jane I'd shoot you down like a dog!'

'We never did her no harm.'

'You had no right messin' with my wife.'

'Not messin',' said Hart. 'Talkin', that was all.'

'She ain't done nothin'.'

Hart nodded. 'And you done too much.'

It was quiet outside now, quiet aside from the occasional shout and the sound of feet running along the sidewalk, the street.

Hart looked at the gunman's pistol. 'Use that and you're dead.'

Hardin almost smiled. 'We're both dead,' he said.

'That what you want?'

'I want you, Ranger. Dead.'

'Enough to die for it?'

The two men stared at one another; everyone else inside the low-ceilinged room seemed to be holding their breath. Hart's mind raced. What had happened to Lefty? What had it to do with Hardin being there in town? What was going to happen now?

Three horses came up the street fast, only two of them with riders. Hart saw the movement back of the gunfighter, the anxiety.

'John, c'mon! Some Ranger's got hisself shot!'

Hart tensed: Hardin bit hard into the flesh of his lower lip.

'John! Now!'

Hardin's breathing was coming heavier; he made two short paces back till he was in the doorway. The pistol was still levelled at Hart's chest. 'One day,' he said with a shake of the head, 'one day I'm goin' to kill you!'

He backed across the sidewalk, covered now by both mounted men. If they had any thought of firing on Hart it didn't survive past their realization that however quick they were he was likely to finish Hardin first.

Hardin didn't look at Hart again until he was in the saddle. Then it was one hasty glance, anger bright in his eyes. Spurs kicked the animal into movement and the gunman was away down the street. The two men flanking him swung round and fired their guns into the ground in front of where Hart stood. Earth and splinters of wood spurted high into the air and Hart didn't budge. For a few seconds his mind was torn, but there was no denying what he had to do. The Colt slotted back into its holster, he set off in the opposite direction, up the street towards the livery stable.

Lefty was lying on the ground, one leg stretched out, the other pulled up towards his stomach. The leg that was straight was torn and bleeding. Part of it seemed to be hanging clear, barely attached. Lefty's arms were pressed across his chest, as though attempting to hold his shattered ribcage in place. Blood seeped through his hands till his fingers were steeped in it.

One of his guns lay on the ground five yards away from his reach; the other was still in its holster.

Hart picked up the loose pistol and spun the chamber, checked how many shells had been fired.

None.

He went down on one knee beside Lefty and turned him on to his back, straightening the bent leg. For some reason that seemed important. He was surprised, though he'd touched recently dead men before, at how warm Lefty's body felt. His hands, the blood-speckled face with its expression of surprise overladen with disbelief.

Aware that there were figures crowded into the doorway yet ignoring them, Hart stared at his friend's face for several moments more. As if waiting for the expression to change. Standing up, he glanced at the unfired gun and wished it not to be like that. There had to be at least a dozen gunshot wounds in Lefty's body and he hadn't been able to squeeze off a single shot. Some fool thought about Paradise showed itself at the edge of Hart's mind and he shook his head to clear it away.

The man with the bad leg was sitting on a hay bale, fingers tracing a slow path up and down the stick.

Hart caught hold of his shirt and hauled him to his feet so hard that he all but tumbled him over. Fear rose fast back of the man's eyes.

'What the hell happened?' Hart shouted, the echo of his voice booming away from the roof. 'What happened here?'

The trail of the three riders had led a little over a mile to the Ross river. Hart tracked the stream for several miles in either direction, checking both sides of the bank, and came up with nothing. In places the hoofmarks were too few, in others too many and mingled with those of cattle crossing. Whoever had ambushed Lefty O'Neal was well clear and settled snug in some shack that could be located anywhere in three counties.

Lefty's dead body was strapped over the back of his horse and wrapped in sacking and a sheet of tarpaulin. He could have been buried in Paradise Spring, but Hart hadn't figured Lefty would have reckoned much to that.

He'd pieced together what he could from the feller in the livery barn and several of the other townsfolk. Rumours that rustlers had been using Paradise Spring as a stopping-off place seemed to have been largely correct. They'd varied in numbers between three and half-a-dozen and it had been no more than chance that a bunch of them had been in town when the Rangers rode in. They'd picked out Hart and Lefty for what they were and made a run for the livery, telling the old timer with the bad leg that if he didn't front for them, they'd shoot the other one so full of lead he'd never be able to walk at all.

Hart rode into Rangers headquarters with the image of Lefty's perplexed face clear before him, almost as definite as the bulk beneath the heavy tarpaulin tied to the trailing horse. Those men who were around stared on in silence, saying nothing nor needing to. There could be only one thing under that cover, only one thing that made that kind of shape. And they knew who Hart had ridden out with.

Captain Armstrong stood in the doorway of his office, leaning one hand against the frame and favouring the leg that had picked up more than its share of gunshot.

His face was a grim mask as he waved a couple of men forward to take charge of Hart's burden. Later there would be a burial detail, men standing stiffly to attention, flags and an oration, words from the good book. Then there would be letters to write, details to be altered, trivia to be attended to. But before all of that he wanted to hear Hart's report.

The Captain motioned Hart into his office and closed the door behind the pair of them.

'Coffee?'

Hart shook his head. 'Let's get it over.'

Armstrong nodded, suppressed a sigh; he pulled some sheets of paper across his desk, selected a pencil, told Hart to sit down and tell it straight as he could. When it was over he tapped the pencil several times on the edge of the desk and stood up. He poured them both mugs of black coffee from the pot which stood on the stove at the back of the room.

'No trace,' he repeated, his eyes fast on Hart's face.

'No.'

'We'll catch up with them.'

Hart nodded. 'Sure.'

'Some day.'

Hart drank some of the coffee. He wanted to tell the Captain about the expression on Lefty O'Neal's face when he'd found him but didn't see how he could. He scraped the chair back and stood up. Armstrong looked at him, half-guessing what he was thinking.

'There ain't no blame, Wes . . .'

Hart nodded. 'Maybe.'

'Comin' up against Hardin that way, there weren't nothin' you could do for Lefty.'

This time Hart didn't say anything.

'Sides, not many folk gazed down the end of John Wesley Hardin's gun an' lived to tell the tale.'

Hart still didn't answer. Armstrong shifted himself round in his chair, the unease getting through to him. He figured that even if Hart had made it out of the saloon when the first shots were fired he'd still have been too late to prevent his colleague being killed. He thought of saying so, spelling it out, but reckoned it was better to let Hart figure it out for himself.

Instead he asked, 'No way Hardin was tied in with them as got the drop on Lefty?'

'Not as far as I could see.'

Armstrong nodded: 'Okay.'

Hart turned to the door.

'Wes.'

'Yeah?'

'That business with Hardin's wife – I reckon he meant what he said, 'bout killin' you for it if he gets the chance.'

'Yeah, I reckon he did.'

Armstrong waited until the echo of the door being shut hard into the frame had subsided. Then he gave a short sigh and reached into one of the drawers of his desk for a stubby cigar. He struck a match and lit the cigar and pulled a few papers towards him and tried to concentrate on what was printed upon them. He'd seen a lot of good men brought back tied across their saddles but that didn't make it one jot easier.

Seven

26 May 1874
Comanche, Texas
The rising thunder of hoofs threatened to be lost in the swell of sound from the cheering, raucous crowd. Of the four horses

that had started, only two were in contention, but they were racing neck and neck up the length of main street, eager for the finish. Both riders were straining forward in their saddles, feet pushed hard into their stirrups. Whips cracked through the air, slashed down against the animals' flanks. Saliva flew from the mouths and nostrils of the horses, sweat lathered their coats. Roan and chestnut: chestnut and roan.

The tape was seventy yards off and seemed a mile away.

Sixty.

Fifty.

A man jumped out from the crowd thronging the sidewalk and held a glass of frothy beer aloft and yelled the roan home. Voices drowned him and hands, angry or merely restraining, hauled him back. The beer splashed into the man's face and down his already-stained shirt front. Others called for both riders to use their whips, their spurs, knock the man alongside clear from the saddle.

Thirty yards and there was still nothing to choose between them; a straw could not have been placed that would have divided them cleanly. The man on the chestnut had his head right over the horse's fine, broad nose as if he was attempting to drag it across the line through his own physical effort. His rival sat slightly further back and worked his whip hard, flicking it from one side to the other so fast that all that could be seen was a blur of fan-like movement.

'Come on, you bastard!'

'Do it, for God's sake!'

'C'mon! C'mon!'

'Sayer! Sayer! Sayer!'

As the chant of his name was roared out, the roan's rider worked his whip even harder and just when it seemed that neither horse could possibly pass the other within the ten yards remaining, the roan somehow found an extra kick, an extra stride.

As it nosed out the chestnut the sound of Sayer's name became lost in a tremendous shout of exaltation like a thunder clap. Already men were leaping off the sidewalk and running to where both horses were now cantering, slowing, beginning to turn. Boots trampled the broken tape into the broken dirt of the street. Faces were charged with excitement, disappointment. The rider of the chestnut leaned well back in his saddle now and tried to avoid the glances, the threats from those who had lost their money, the occasional cries of sympathy and condolence. Mostly the crowd broke around him and reformed in its dash towards the winner.

Arms reached out towards Sayer and lifted him bodily from the saddle, hoisted him shoulder-high and proceeded to parade him down the street in the direction of the saloon. The horse's owner, three hundred dollars better off, looked with a certain touch of bitterness at the bloody weals on the roan's sweating coat before ordering one of his men to lead the horse to the stable and tend to her. That settled, he readjusted his hat, fidgeted his cravat into position and followed the triumphant party through the losers and the mere onlookers.

Some yards off, a younger man hailed him and, hand still raised in greeting, stepped off the sidewalk towards him.

The pair shook hands warmly, clasping arms.

'You had your coat on her, I hope, John?'

'Coat an' hat an' britches.'

'That's good. You're comin' to celebrate victory?'

'I've been celebrating all day,' the young man laughed.

The owner raised an eyebrow and looked at him carefully. 'You were that certain, John, my roan would win?'

'It's not that. Though I was sure enough about your horse. But today's my birthday.'

'I'm damned if it is!'

'Twenty-one,' John Wesley Hardin laughed. 'Twenty-one and a damn sight richer now than I was when the day started.'

'Ain't we both?' exclaimed the horse owner, 'ain't we both.'

They laughed and Hardin called over his friends and introduced them: there were three of the Dixon boys, Bill, Bud and Tom, Jim Taylor, and John Wesley's own brother, Joe Hardin.

The men swopped versions of the race a while and then Jim Taylor asked why they were standing around in the street and talking when they could be doing it much more comfortably inside the saloon.

Nobody came up with a good reason so they swaggered off in the direction of the Lone Star.

As they approached the already swinging batwing doors, Joe Hardin stood aside and waited for his brother, intercepting him and saying quietly, 'You don't think maybe we should take our winnin's and do our drinkin' elsewhere?'

John Wesley allowed more than a hint of anger to glint in his pale eyes; the taut skin of his handsome, moustached face tightened over his cheekbones even further.

'What the hell you talkin' 'bout?' Unsurprisingly, John Wesley's voice showed signs of slurring. He had been drinking and celebrating since before breakfast, egged on by his friends to make his twenty-first birthday an occasion to remember.

Joe hesitated, but went ahead anyhow, his hand blocking his brother from stepping on to the sidewalk. 'You know that bastard Webb's in town?'

John Wesley shook his head, as if to clear it. 'So what?'

'You know he's sworn to get you for what you done to Morgan?'

John Wesley laughed aloud. 'Charlie Webb ain't comin' near me! Not today. Not any day.' He jabbed his brother with his index finger. 'He sure ain't fool enough to try nothin' with all you boys around. Is he, now?'

John Wesley draped an arm about Joe's shoulders and turned towards the saloon. 'There's champagne in there, Joe, and it's waitin' for some fine person to call a toast to my health. Let's quit fartin' around and get to it!'

Joe held his tongue and allowed himself to be propelled through the doors towards the cheer of greeting that met them on the other side. Jim Taylor held the magnum of champagne between his legs and pushed the cork free with both thumbs. There was a single crack like gunfire and the cork flew high towards the smoke-ringed ceiling. Someone pushed a glass into John Wesley's hand and Taylor filled it past the brim, champagne running down on to the floor.

'Easy! Easy!' John Wesley shouted. 'I don't want no bath in the stuff!'

'Then drink it down, why don't you? Make room for some more. We got a whole crate over there wants takin' care of.'

A roar of laughter and encouragement went up as Hardin finished the contents of the glass and held it towards Jim Taylor to be refilled. Soon they were sitting at a table on the low balcony, a bunch of rowdy, raucous men with nothing on their mind but getting drunk and making as much noise as they knew how doing it.

'Don't you wish Jane were here, John?' asked his brother at one point.

Hardin grinned and shook his head and carried on leering at the woman in a red fur-trimmed dress who was sitting close to the downstairs bar.

They were just about half-way through their crate of champagne when a skinny feller wearing spectacles and a long, threadbare coat pushed his way through the batwing doors and blinked across through the smoke. He adjusted to the noise and the light and then filtered his way between the raceday crowd, heading towards the bar.

For answer to his question, the bartender looked at him sharply and then cast his eyes high at the rear of the room.

The skinny man nodded and wet his lips and took a couple of paces away from the counter. He hesitated, turned, patted his side pocket. The two dollar pieces Deputy Sheriff Webb had given him jangled against one another. He took one out and fingered it down on to the bar top, trying to avoid the patches of wet that were almost everywhere.

'Change your mind?' asked the barkeep.

The man fidgeted with his glasses and said: 'Whisky.'

His voice was so low and the clamour so loud, the bartender had to ask him to repeat it twice.

It took the man some little time to down his whisky, the burn of it strong enough to bring tears to his eyes. The bartender seemed to be using the excuse of the largely drunken crowd for ridding his supplies of whatever inferior stock he had – and there was plenty.

'Thanks,' said the skinny man to no one in particular.

No one heard him.

He fussed with the sides of his spectacles some more and set off towards the back of the saloon. He blinked along the table, trying to figure out which of the three younger men with moustaches was the one he had the message for.

Finally, he sidled up close to a girl in a red dress and leaned towards the man at her back. 'You John Wesley Hardin?' he asked.

Bud Dixon hollered with laughter, spittle splashing off his tongue into the man's face.

'You got the wrong boy,' he called. 'He's right there in the middle. It's his party, ain't it?'

The skinny man backed off a couple of feet, removed his glasses and wiped the spray off on to his sleeve, set them back on his thin nose and asked the woman to excuse him.

After three attempts she still didn't seem to have heard him, so he resorted to squeezing past her, with the result that she jabbed an elbow into his midriff and asked him what the hell he thought he was doing.

The man apologized and said he was trying to get to Mr Hardin.

'Which Mr Hardin?' asked the man who was stroking the woman's arm.

'Mr John Wesley Hardin.'

The hand ceased stroking and reached out fast, grabbing one side of the long coat and pulling its owner down to the table. Glasses spilt and shouts roared. Hardin laughed and swayed and hauled the man even closer, dragging him to his knees, the frightened bespectacled face inches from his own.

'Wha' is it?'

'Message. I got . . . message.'

'Who from?'

'Sheriff.'

Hardin thrust the face away to arm's length, stared at it as if suddenly meaningful then pulled it sharply back, nearly sending the man's glasses off his nose.

'What sheriff?'

'Webb. Sheriff . . .'

'Charlie Webb.'

'Yeah.'

John Wesley Hardin reached round for a drink, found his own glass was empty and took Jim Taylor's. Empty, he passed it back.

'What the hell's he want?'

'He said . . .' faltered the man.

'Yeah, c'mon, spit it out. What the fuck's he say?'

'Wants to see you. Talk. No . . . no tricks. No gunplay. That's what . . .'

But Hardin had stopped listening. He was on his feet, waving his arms to shut the others up, the woman in the red dress forgotten, his drunkenness already falling away, as if it had been a comfortable coat he had borrowed and worn for a while but could now cast aside.

'You hear that? You hear that?' He pointed from one man round the table to another. 'There's someone out there wants to speak to me. Wants a talk. Friendly little talk.' Hardin winked broadly. 'No gunplay an' no tricks, ain't that right?'

He grabbed hold of the skinny man's arm and twisted it behind his back, the man's face banging hard against the table, one of the lenses of his spectacles cracking across but remaining in its frame.

'Ain't that right?' Hardin demanded. 'No tricks an' no guns. Ain't that what you said?'

The messenger tried to answer but with his face forced into the table, all he could manage was a few muffled grunts.

Hardin pulled him away and pushed him staggering away from the table. The man grasped hold of the balcony rail and hung there for several moments.

Joe Hardin went over to him and asked him where Webb wanted the meeting to take place.

'Hanney Devlin's,' replied the man, catching his breath.

'When?' called Jim Taylor.

'He's there now. I'm to . . . to tell him if you're comin'.'

Taylor laughed. 'I'll tell you what you can tell Charlie Webb – you can—'

'You can tell him I'll be there.'

All the men stared at John Wesley, for a moment silent. Then, when they raised their voices in urgent protest, he called over the top of them, 'Tell him I'll be right over. In just as much time as it takes to finish off another bottle of champagne.'

The skinny messenger nodded and scrambled his way down the stairs and towards the door. The news followed in his wake and rumour and counter-rumour spread through the saloon and out on to the street. Someone was taking bets and offering Hardin better odds than the favourite that afternoon.

'You're jokin', John,' said Jim Taylor, moving his chair alongside Hardin. 'You'd be walking into a trap.'

'I ain't afraid of Webb. He's been shootin' his mouth off about what he's plannin' to do to me for long enough. Now I'm goin' to face him out an' show folk he ain't nothin' but wind an' water.'

Hardin stood up and Taylor stood with him, closing on him further. 'No one's saying you're afraid. Just this ain't the right time. You know what Devlin's place is, well as I do. It'll be packed with Sutton's cronies an' trash like that. You can't walk in there.'

For a moment, Taylor thought that Hardin was going to throw a punch at him. But John Wesley bit down his anger and turned away from Taylor, pushing the table back to force his way through.

'I'm takin' a walk along to Hanney Devlin's,' he announced. 'Take a drink with my friend Charlie Webb. Who's comin' with me?'

Without waiting to see which of the men would follow, Hardin went briskly down the steps and through the saloon, brushing off the advice and concern of well-wishers on his way to the door. Once in the street, he looked over his shoulder and saw the two Dixon boys, Bud and Tom, as well as his own brother, Joe. John

Wesley's face clouded over, seeing that Jim Taylor had decided to let him go in without his gun to back him up. Well, he'd show him!

There were a few stragglers outside Devlin's and a crowd packing out the doorway which broke inside when Hardin and the three other men neared the entrance. John Wesley hardly hesitated on his way into the low-ceilinged saloon and eating house. The door had no time to swing back before Deputy Sheriff Webb was walking through a bunch of onlookers to greet him.

'Hardin, I heard you was comin' over.'

'You wanted to talk.'

Webb held out his hand and Hardin didn't even glance at it. After a couple of seconds, Webb pulled the hand back with a tight-lipped smile and invited Hardin over to his table for a drink.

'Fine,' said John Wesley, 'only we're drinkin' champagne.'

Webb shook his head with a laugh. 'Hanney don't run to champagne. But his whisky's better'n most. Come on over and try some.'

Hardin shrugged his shoulders, glanced at the expectant crowd, and followed Webb to a table close to the centre of the room. There were three others sitting there, only one of whom Hardin recognized. Inside the place were several of Sutton's men, he knew that for certain, but with his brother and the Dixons to back him up and a quantity of champagne inside him, he felt confident enough.

'You had your shirt on the winner today,' said Webb, passing the bottle in Hardin's direction.

John Wesley waited for a clean glass, then poured himself a good shot, passing on the bottle to Joe.

'Shirt and suit, the lot,' he agreed. 'It's been a good day.'

'I'm sure it has.'

'An' it's John's birthday,' said Joe Hardin, beginning to relax.

Charlie Webb pushed back his chair at the news. He raised his glass and made a brief speech in Hardin's honour, asking everyone to join him in a toast to the young man's health.

'Long life to you,' said Webb, staring directly at him.

John Wesley lifted his own glass. 'And to you, Charlie,' he said. 'And to you.'

For ten or fifteen minutes they gossiped about horses and cattle and the tension seemed to be evaporating; hangers-on around the saloon lost interest and wandered back to the bar or stood close by the various card games in progress. Heads that had been peering over the door disappeared. Webb stretched back in his chair, one booted foot resting on the edge of the table. A fresh bottle had been summoned from the bar. Then while the others were engaged in the merits of the afternoon's riders, Webb leaned forward and spoke to Hardin quietly. Quietly, yet there was no mistaking the edge of steel to his voice.

'We didn't mention what happened in Albuquerque, John.'

Hardin's eyes narrowed. 'What about it?'

'That business with Helm, that was a bad business.'

'For Helm,' John Wesley agreed.

'For the territory, John. A sworn office of the law being gunned down in the execution of his duty.'

'Sworn officer of the law in a pig's ass! An' the only execution on Jack Helm's mind was mine.'

Webb shook his head, still leaning across the table, still keeping his voice low. 'That ain't true, John. There's witnesses. Them as'll swear to Helm's intentions.'

Hardin pulled back with a snort. 'Witnesses! I bet you got witnesses who'll swear to any damn thing you pay 'em to say.'

The other conversation had mostly stopped now, men were watching Hardin and Webb; those close to the table silent and anxious.

'Now, John,' Webb continued, still soft in voice, 'I thought we were here to talk about this man to man, discuss this as sensible folk and try to find some way of resolving the difficulties. It ain't no use your goin' off that way an' losin' your temper.'

Hardin stared at the sheriff, hating the man's reasonable manner, the smile about his eyes and mouth and the treachery he was certain lay behind them.

'See, John,' Webb continued calmly, 'if you an' me can't find a way to talk this out, then there's got to be other ways.'

'Meanin' what, Charlie?' asked Hardin.

Webb slid his hands along the table. Shrugged lightly. 'Other ways,' he repeated.

Hardin's eye was caught by a movement back of Webb's shoulder, someone pushing through the tables with a purpose. He glanced quickly round and thought he recognized one of Webb's deputies no more than a dozen or so feet from his back. As Hardin's head swung away, he caught the quick, almost imperceptible movement of hand towards gun.

Other ways.

'Joe,' yelled Hardin, 'it's a trap!'

Someone hollered loud and Hardin sprang to his feet, fingers diving for his .44. Charlie Webb didn't try to rise; he arched himself backwards and pulled his pistol up from its holster. Both men seemed to fire at the same time. A slug ripped its way through John Wesley's side, close above his left hip. Webb was smashed out of his chair with blood pouring from a wound above his temple.

'John ! John! Get out!'

Jim Taylor had knocked one of Webb's deputies unconscious and forced his way in through the rear. Bill Dixon alongside him, he ploughed through the crowd, gun drawn. Another of Webb's men turned to face him and Taylor smacked him hard in the mouth with the barrel of his gun. The man went down spitting blood and fragments of broken tooth.

Charlie Webb was on all fours, blood leaking from his head.

Shouting filled the saloon.

John Wesley was midway between where he'd been sitting and the street door. The man he'd seen reaching for his gun before seemed to have melted back into the crowd.

'Bastard!' yelled Jim Taylor. 'Lyin' bastard!'

He lashed out his boot at Webb, kicking one of his arms away from under him. As Webb fell towards the floor, Taylor put a bullet into the back of his head from close range. Bill Dixon watched the pulped grey splash against his pants leg and laughed, thumbing back the hammer and firing into Webb's back and sides.

The dead man's limbs jerked hard and his boots hammered the floor.

John Wesley tried to see what was going down; he saw Jim Taylor waving him away; saw someone throwing a punch at his brother, Joe, and connecting with the side of his jaw. He tried to move back towards him, but found his path blocked. He turned and a punch landed low in his stomach and he doubled forward. A blow aimed at his head and narrowly missed. Several others had their guns out now and were firing indiscriminately.

A hand seized John Wesley's arm and he whirled round but it was Jim Taylor.

'Thought you weren't comin'.'

'Save your breath,' called Taylor. 'There's horses out front.'

'Joe . . .' Hardin began, swinging round.

The glass mirror behind the bar shattered into a hundred pieces. A shotgun was discharged over the heads of the crowd. John Wesley saw his brother going down under pummelling fists. Neither of the young Dixon boys seemed to have extricated themselves from the centre of the crowd. Jim Taylor was still hauling on his arm. A pistol swung close to his head, missed and struck his shoulder instead, numbing the bone. He tried to bring up his own gun but his arm was knocked aside.

'Now, John! Now!'

John Wesley kicked one man in the leg, elbowed another in the face. He found room to swing his pistol and lashed the sight across a man's cheek, tearing the skin apart.

He went through the door as a rifle started firing from across the street. He paused long enough to send a covering shot and then grabbed for the reins that Taylor was handing down to him. One boot in the stirrup and he dropped his gun into the holster, slapped the horse hard on the rump. As it started to gallop down the street. John Wesley swung his leg over and settled low in the saddle, head right down by the animal's neck.

Bullets whined through the air above and around them as

they drove the horses away, making as much speed as the pair that had raced along the same street a few hours earlier.

Eight

January 1875

The lean-to had never been finished. All it contained now was some three feet of snow, wedged tight. The front of the house was spotted with more snow and the edges of the windows were covered in ice. Part of the fence had been blown down by the wind and what remained was leaning at a perilous angle to the ground. The only things standing in the garden were two sticks, set there to support some growth or other, and left.

Wes Hart swung down from the saddle and looped the rein over one of the surviving pieces of fencing. He slapped his arms back and forth across his body, clearing away the snow that the northerly had blown against him. He wore the Indian blanket over his coat, a wool scarf was wound about his neck and the lower part of his face. A length of string kept his flat-brimmed hat clamped tight on his head. Scuffed leather gloves failed to keep the cold from biting at his hands.

The last time he'd come visiting at the Hardin place Lefty O'Neal had been with him. Now Lefty was dead: a lot of men were dead. Hart stepped through the gap in the fence where the gate had once been and walked briskly towards the door. This time there was no rifle barrel poking through the sacking at the side window and if it hadn't been for the trail of chimney smoke he'd been seeing for the best part of a mile, he might have figured that Jane Hardin had quit Comanche County along with her husband.

His knock on the door shifted a film of snow down its face.

A voice called for him to wait.

When the door opened, Jane Hardin was wearing shawl and coat and holding a small girl close to her side, the child's hands lost inside the thick folds of her mother's long dress.

'What is it?' She sounded weary, her eyes like her voice were filled with tiredness, a lack of sleep.

'Just a few words, Mrs Hardin.'

Hart wondered if she recognized him, but the next thing she said made it clear that she did.

'John said he'd kill you for coming bothering me when he was gone.'

Hart looked at her. 'He's killed a lot of folk.'

She stared back at him and didn't say anything. The girl started to murmur and Jane pushed her fingers into her long, fair hair.

'Shut the door,' she told Hart. 'Keep the warmth in.'

He did as he was told and then unfastened the string and pulled off his hat, hanging it from one of the wooden pegs at the back of the door. He removed the blanket, snow falling across the floor as he did so. The colours were dark, subdued, the patterns all but lost.

'Take off that coat, too,' she said. 'Set it to warm close by the fire.'

Hart did so, noticing now that the little girl had moved away that Hardin's wife was once again with child.

'There's a piece of pie on the stove,' the woman said, turning her head.

'There ain't no need . . .'

'I was brung up hospitable.'

Hart nodded, albeit grudgingly. 'Okay, Mrs Hardin, I'd be obliged.'

'An' coffee?'

She was already reaching the thick china cup down from the dresser and carrying it towards the bubbling pot. Hart realized that she had let her hair grow longer and now the ends touched the nape of her neck and were beginning to curl.

'You know he ain't been here this long time,' she said, handing him the cup.

Hart nodded, tasted the coffee; it was hot and strong. The little girl clung again to her mother's skirts, staring at him, big-eyed. Jane Hardin cut a wide slice of pie and pushed it on to a tin plate. Before she gave it to Hart, she cut away a small piece, hardly more than a sliver, and handed it down to the girl.

'Won't you sit down?'

She gestured towards the thick wood table and Hart pulled out a stool and sat up to it, accepting the plate and a fork. The pie was made from apples saved from the summer, wrapped in cloth at the back of a drawer.

Jane hesitated a while, fussed over the little girl's hair. 'If you knew my husband weren't here . . .'

'I was passin' close,' Hart said.

She shook her head. 'Don't treat me like a fool.'

'I wasn't . . .'

'Because I ain't.'

He sighed, eased the plate away. 'Okay. I'm sorry. I figured if I come by you might know where he was.'

'And tell you?' she asked incredulously.

Hart forked into the pie and lifted a section to his mouth, washing it down a few moments later with coffee. The fire sparked up and the little girl oohed and tensed and then cuddled down into her mother's lap, head between her breasts. Jane Hardin glanced at Hart and he looked back at her and for a while there was silence between them.

He finished the pie and she reached across for the plate, rousing her daughter to carry it to the bucket that waited alongside the stove. Feeling was beginning to seep back into Hart's toes and finger ends, making them tingle. He cupped the coffee in his hands and drank.

'You didn't really think I'd inform on my own husband?'

'No, ma'am. Not really. Only . . .'

'What?'

'He seems to have left you to fend for yourself a long time.'

'That don't mind.'

Hart turned his head to one side. 'Woman alone, out here in winter, that's hard.'

She made a little shaking motion with her head. 'What else d'you think a woman's life is in this country?'

Hart nodded. 'A man can make it easier.'

'Yeah. An' he can make it a damn sight harder.'

He looked full at her. 'Which of them's your man done?'

Jane Hardin gave him her back; she rinsed the plate in the ice-cold water of the bucket and stood it on the dresser.

'Are you married?' she asked several moments later.

'Uh-uh.'

'Maybe if you were you'd understand better.'

'My father, he died when I was three years old. When I was five my mother married again, an Irishman who gave her three daughters and another son, one after another. I know when life's hard for a woman.'

'She had you to help her.'

Hart started to say something but fell quiet. He didn't want to try and explain to this woman how he had tried to help his mother at the birth of Sean, her last-born. He didn't want to explain to the wife of a wanted killer how his mother had begun bleeding so heavily he had been terrified – eleven years of age – and had frozen with fear. How she had called and called for help and there had been nothing he could do. He had not dared to go closer, to touch her. All that blood!

When at last he had arrived back with their nearest neighbour, his mother had been dead, the child, almost miraculously, alive.

The dirt had been over his mother's grave some six weeks before his stepfather had returned home.

And here was Jane Hardin, heavily pregnant while her husband was in hiding, probably in some other county, even out of the state.

She studied his silence, realized he was looking at her swollen belly and said: 'He's sending for me. In time, John's sending for me. It'll be all right.'

Hart nodded curtly. 'If he doesn't?'

'He will.' Her voice sounded as though she believed it, her

eyes testified that she believed it. But her fingers opened and closed nervously inside the fall of her skirt.

'When I was here last,' Hart said, 'you told me your husband didn't have no choice but to kill Jack Helm.'

'That's right. Nor did he.'

'How 'bout Deputy Webb – that the same?'

She pulled at the shawl a trace too hastily. 'Of course. Webb was in Sutton's pocket. He lured John into a trap. If he hadn't shot his way out of there, they would have gunned him down.'

'Mrs Hardin, he never had to walk in there.'

'Why shouldn't he go where he wants?' demanded Jane Hardin, anger beginning to spark her eyes.

'He walked into a bar crammed full of Sutton men. He knew that.'

'Why would John . . .?'

'He did it because he'd been drinking heavy and winnin' heavy on the horses and he was feelin' more pleased with himself than usual. He did it because he knew Webb was workin' some kind of trap and he figured he'd look pretty big in the eyes of his friends if he stepped right into it.'

'I don't believe you.'

'Suit yourself. But the way I see it, your man acted out of stubborn foolishness an' bravado and on account of that Charlie Webb got shot through the head, several others got bad wounded and three men got hanged.'

She stared at him, jolted off course. 'Hanged!'

'Sure. Just something it looks like your beloved John Wesley forgot to mention.'

Jane Hardin leaned across the table, staring at him. 'Who was hanged?'

'Couple of the Dixon brothers. And a young feller named Joe – maybe you got to meet him at your wedding.'

Jane went pale. Her hands gripped the table hard and her daughter began to whimper, sensing something was wrong and not understanding what.

'He didn't tell you.'

She shook her head slowly, lips parted.

'Maybe he didn't reckon it was too important.'

Jane Hardin grasped the china cup and aimed it at Hart's head. He ducked inside it easily, catching at her arm as she followed through, fingers flailing for his face.

They were both leaning across the corner of the table, swaying slightly, their breathing forced and heavy. The girl tugged at her mother and started to cry, not understanding what was happening, but knowing that it was frightening. A trace of spittle showed at one side of Jane Hardin's face; her eyes were wide with anger.

Hart waited. Then said: 'Him and Jim Taylor galloped out of town and left 'em to be stretched. It weren't nice. Nothing legal. Just a mob.' He released her arm. 'If they hadn't tied hemp round their neck, they'd've torn 'em to pieces with their hands.' He stood back. 'There's them as reckon your husband uses his gun in a right cause, but there weren't many of them there that day.'

Jane controlled her breathing, shushed her child. For a few seconds a wave of nausea swept through her and she thought she would vomit. Her mind swung round. Hart moved fast enough to catch her before she hit the floor. The child crying and beating at his legs with little fists, he lifted the woman into his arms and carried her through the sacking partition and laid her on the quilt-covered bed.

The he reached down and picked up the little girl and tried to tell her that her mother would be all right if they allowed her to rest quiet for a time and didn't fuss.

When Jane Hardin came round, no more than minutes later, the width of sacking was pulled back and she could see Hart and her daughter sitting on opposite sides of the table, eyeing one another with suspicion.

As soon as he saw she had come to, Hart took her a glass of water which she accepted with a slight nod of the head and sipped cautiously before levering herself round on the bed and touching her feet to the floor. The child ran to her and lost her face alongside the swelling belly.

'Why don't you go?' Jane said, not looking at him.

'I'll stay a while till you're feelin' better.'

Then she did look at him and already some of the heat was back in her eyes. 'I am better!'

Hart continued to look at her, all the while remembering the expression of pain on his mother's face as she lay back with her legs forced high and the bed got redder and redder.

'Please go! Leave us.'

He nodded and stood up, reaching for his coat, the Indian blanket, his hat. The child peeped out at him from under one arm. Only at the door did he pause and turn.

'Those friends of his,' Hart said, 'he'll need them to stand by him now. There's four thousand dollars on his head. That sort of money can win over a whole lot of people.'

He went out fast, shutting the door hard, slamming out the hate in her eyes. It was misting with snow and the wind had changed direction, shifting towards the west. It had been a long time since he'd wished maybe he had a woman of his own, but God he was wishing it then.

Hart had no way of knowing that before that new year was out he'd meet Kathy: nor that before John Wesley Hardin was finally taken prisoner, she would have left him again.

Nine

Late summer 1876

Ollie Halverton leaned his skinny body against the door frame and watched the boy turning the onions round the skillet. No more than twelve or thirteen and not above average height for his age, he stood on a wooden box set close by the stove, never taking his eyes off what he was doing. As the onions began to brown, he reached over to where the pork chop was resting in the bottom of a thick pan and dropped it amongst the onions with a splash of fat. The smell that hissed up into the doorway made Ollie's mouth all but slaver.

'Let him get on with it without you starin' at him, Ollie,' called Lamar from the main room. 'Won't taste no better for havin' to see your miserable face.'

'You hush up your tongue, Lamar,' said Ollie with a pretence at anger. 'I'm just lookin' after our interests, that's all.'

'What you got in there, steak or gold workin's? That don't need no watchin'.'

The chop was turned on to its other side and the fat hissed; the boy moved the onions off to one side of the skillet and reached over for the bowl of fresh-laid eggs.

'Two or three?' he asked without turning his head.

Ollie's tongue moved around the edges of his mouth. 'Three,' he said, smiling. 'Three looks about fine.'

'Three what?' called Lamar. 'Three steaks?'

'I ain't eatin' steak. You're the one who's havin' steak.'

'Three what, then?'

'I'm takin' the pork chop,' said Ollie with relish.

'Three pork chops?' asked Lamar, amazed.

Ollie shook his head in desperation. 'Three eggs.' He jutted his index finger at the other Ranger. 'You want eggs on your steak?'

'Course I do.'

'How many?'

Lamar grinned. 'Couple.'

Ollie nodded and called in to the boy, 'Two eggs on the steak.'

The boy already had them in the pan. A couple of minutes later he lifted out steak and chop, eggs and onions and slid them on to a couple of plates. He used a ladle to set portions of beans on to each plate, reached for four thick slices of cornbread and somehow found a space for them as well. They were big plates.

He carried them through from the kitchen, one balanced on

the palm of either small hand, Ollie watching him closely, sure that the boy must drop one or the other or both before he reached the table. Of course, he dropped neither.

Lamar wiped at his heavily bearded mouth by way of expectation and leaned forward in his chair. Ollie waited until the boy had stepped back from the table and slid into his seat fast.

'Damn!' he said with a deal of feeling. 'Don't that look good?'

'Uh!' Lamar grunted, cutting a chunk a couple of inches square off the end of the steak. 'Uh-huh!'

The meat was half-way to his mouth when they heard footsteps coming fast along the side alley that led to the dining room door. Lamar glanced at Ollie, dropped his fork and reached for his pistol. Ollie scraped back his chair and started to stand, his hand making the move for his own gun.

Hart stood inside the open door, glanced at the other diners, saw the two Rangers and took a couple of paces towards them. Lamar and Ollie forgot about their guns, started to relax.

'C'mon,' said Hart urgently. 'Let's ride!'

'Ride!' echoed Ollie loudly. 'Ride! Now! We just . . .' He stared at the food on his plate, unable to say more.

Lamar picked up his fork, the piece of steak still attached, a little blood and juice dripping slowly from it. 'Ain't we got time . . .?'

'No! It's now. He's pinned down about three miles north of town.'

'Who?' asked Ollie, looking regretfully back at his pork chop.

'Who's so all-fired important?' asked Lamar, squashing his stetson down on to his head.

Hart spoke without looking back at either man, intent on getting to his horse. 'Hardin,' he said. 'John Wesley Hardin.'

The cabin was through a sparsely wooded hollow and then some hundred yards up the uneven side of a scrub hill. Back of it were a few trees making a pretty unconvincing job of spreading their branches generously over the angled sod roof. The place itself was the usual notched-log building, low and long, with a couple of uneven rectangles hewn out for windows and a warped door that leaned a few inches to one side. The only thing around the shack was a stout but crooked post around four feet high which looked as if it could have been used as a hitching post. There wasn't anything tied to it right then. The only horse that might have been, a big old creature with a white blaze down its head and an almost-white tail, lay dead in its own blood. From the way the flies were humming round it, the animal had been like that for some little time. It looked to have been gutshot with a shotgun from pretty close range. It stank.

The three Texas Rangers had tethered their own mounts down in the hollow and clambered up to see what was going on. They were met by a crowd of glory boys out for the reward, one Comanche County deputy, a couple of men who claimed to be state policemen but didn't hurry to show any proof, and a pair of Mexicans whom Lamar recognized as running with some of the Sutton crew.

Hart figured if he had to talk with anyone, then it had best be the deputy. He'd far rather have cleared the whole mess of them out and gone about things his own way. That was about as likely as getting invited to the state governor's thanksgiving dinner, so he did what he could.

The deputy was an anxious-seeming man with a hare lip and more weapons than any three usually carried. Aside from the sawn-off Remington 0-0 gauge shotgun which had likely finished off the dead horse, he had a Winchester rifle in his other hand, two pistols holstered at either side of his belt, one more pushed down into his pants and a Bowie knife in a sheath at his back.

'Got an army in there?' asked Hart, glancing obviously at all the armament and then over towards the shack.

'Five, six of 'em. Maybe more.'

Lamar pointed at the men who were mostly hunkered down behind the rim of land that made an irregular semi-circle in front of the shack. There was a spread of open ground between the rim and the building, maybe fifty yards at its farthest point.

'You got the men,' he said. 'Why don't you rush 'em?'

'We did,' said the deputy. 'Didn't do too well.'

'How come?'

'Stopped a couple of bullets,' he nodded to his left. 'They won't go head-on in again, I doubt. Besides, they can't seem to make their minds up as to who's givin' the orders.'

'That's easy,' said Ollie quickly. 'We are.'

The deputy scowled at him and seemed about to argue, but thought better of it and kicked his heel into the ground instead.

'We was told Hardin was in there,' said Hart, 'that's the story got back to town.'

'Why else d'you reckon all these rats come out like some vigilante posse?' the deputy asked, looking around him. 'They ain't interested in nothin' but the reward.'

'Hell!' exclaimed Lamar. 'What you out here for? Justice?'

The hare lip pushed out and the man's eyes narrowed, but still he didn't say anything in return. Three Rangers was clearly more than he liked to handle, even with all that weaponry on him.

Hart and Ollie had moved a few feet away and were studying the shack. Rushing it was asking for trouble, right enough, but getting round back of it wasn't easy without being spotted. One man could do it, though, as long as he was careful and didn't get too impatient. If he could get on to the roof, it ought to be possible to drive at least some of them out. The less guns there were inside, the less covering fire they could give.

'How 'bout it?' said Hart with the beginnings of a grin at the corners of his mouth.

'Why me?' asked Ollie.

'Because you're less of a target than I am?'

'Uh-uh.'

'Okay. Because Lamar an' me got a year's more service than you.'

Ollie shrugged resignedly. 'That I can't argue with. I'll tell you one thing, though. I don't fancy opening that place up just so a bunch of no-goods and bounty hunters can drag Hardin off and string him up from the nearest cottonwood an' claim the reward.'

Hart agreed. 'Let's get 'em together. Spell it out.'

They called the men back down towards the hollow, leaving Lamar behind to keep watch for any signs of a break. He sent the occasional shot skimming off the walls to give the occupants something to think about.

'Whoever's in there,' said Hart meantime, 'John Wesley Hardin or anybody else, they come under our jurisdiction. We take 'em in. You fellers want to stay around and lend a hand, that's fine. But we're givin' the orders and you're obeying 'em. Otherwise it's a ride back to town and that's all you got comin' to you.'

Murmurs and grumbles and a lot of pained faces showed Hart his speech hadn't gone down too well. He glanced at Ollie, both of them conscious that there were a dozen men there and that if they decided to take matters into their own hands, there might be trouble.

Hart picked out the one who was making the most noise – a hefty half-breed Mexican with crossed gun-belts and a spreading gut that was giving the buttons at the front of his shirt a lot of trouble.

Hart got to him smartly and asked him good and loud what he was bellyaching about.

The breed hung his lip and scratched his stomach and told Hart he didn't have any right to come riding in after they'd spent a day and a night chasing Hardin down and steal all the glory. Not to mention the reward.

When he'd said his piece it was pretty quiet.

Everyone was looking at Hart to see how he'd take it.

He made good and sure they all were before showing them.

He was a couple of feet away from the half-breed before the man had even thought about moving. Hart's left hand was already bunched into a fist and he drove it hard into the man's spreading gut. There was little swing to the punch, little back-lift, but it jolted him back gasping open-mouthed as his head jerked forward and down. Hart swayed back on his heels and this time he allowed himself the room to whip his right arm well back before bringing it back on to the side of the breed's jaw.

There was a solid sound, bone on bone, and the man's head wrenched sideways on his neck and his eyes jammed shut. Hart opened them again with a stiff-fingered poke under the adam's apple.

Eyes opened sure enough – hands clawed at the fleshy throat and a scream shrieked out.

Only then did Hart draw his Colt. It moved from holster to hand so fast that most of those watching failed to follow the movement. The gun was simply there, its barrel tip less than six inches away from the breed's gasping, pain-stricken face.

The triple click of the hammer sounded awfully loud. To the breed it was the loudest sound he had ever heard.

Hart rested the gun against the man's forehead and told him to open his eyes. The breed complied only slowly and as soon as he did so his lips began to move almost soundlessly in prayer.

'No rights, huh?' Hart said, and he looked around the watching men. 'No rights?'

The half-breed was still praying, staring at the barrel of the Colt like he was hypnotized. Hart stepped away and slowly and deliberately released the hammer. The breed collapsed to his knees and clutched his stomach, murmuring and mumbling.

'Any of you,' said Hart, turning his head slowly, 'think they want to do this their own way best say so now. Otherwise, you take orders from us.' He slipped the pistol back down into its holster. 'You want to ride out, that's fine by me. If you want to stay, that's fine too. Just remember what I said.'

No one was likely to forget: what Hart had said or what he'd done.

'All right, Ollie,' Hart called a moment later, 'let's make it now,'

Ollie gestured acknowledgment and moved off in the direction of the trees. Hart eased himself up alongside Lamar while half a dozen men mounted up and rode off in search of easier pickings. The rest resumed their positions around the broken rim of land.

'You reckon he's in there?' asked Lamar.

Hart shook his head. 'Who knows? Some of this crew've

been chasin' someone long and hard. They think Hardin's in there.'

Lamar laughed roughly. 'Some of these buzzards'd chase their own grandmothers for bein' Hardin in disguise, they want the reward money so bad.'

'Yeah. I guess you're right. Damn rewards are more trouble'n they're worth half the time. Bounty hunters all over the country. Folks givin' information that proves to be a pack of lies when you follow it up.'

Lamar laughed again. 'You remember that feller who tried to convince us he'd got Hardin trapped in his loft and all the time it was some half-crazed cowpoke who'd been slippin' it to his wife an' he found out. Wanted us to bust in there and blast him to kingdom-come.'

'You reckon that's what this is?'

Lamar shrugged. 'We'll know soon enough. Ollie should be round there by now.' He slid his rifle further forward on the ground and levered a shell into the breech.

Hart elbowed forward a foot or so and cupped his hands round his mouth: 'You hear me in there?'

His voice was loud across the space between the waiting men and the shack, loud and oddly flat. Whether they heard or not, there was no reply.

'You know we got the place surrounded. We can starve you out or blast you out, it don't make no difference. Either way you ain't got no chance.'

He paused for a couple of moments and one of the men off to his left said, 'We tried talkin' 'em out. You're wastin' your breath.'

Hart ignored him. 'We're Texas Rangers. Surrender to us an' we'll guarantee you safe conduct an' fair trial. There won't be any lynchin'.'

Gun metal glinted at the bottom corner of one of the irregular windows and a couple of shots raked the air above Hart's head. They'd been listening right enough – they just hadn't taken to what he'd had to say.

Hart levered himself back. 'Spotted Ollie yet?'

Lamar nodded. 'Tree back of the roof. Here he comes now.'

Ollie set foot carefully on the sod roof, pistol in hand. He moved cautiously towards the hole centre and rear through which smoke was allowed to escape. Could be that one time there'd been some kind of stove pipe sticking up there, but now there was nothing but a funnel of dark which gradually lightened as his eyes became accustomed to it.

'You got your last chance!' Hart called.

His reply this time came from both windows, one lucky shot well wide of himself but nicking another man on the elbow and causing him to yell and let loose his weapon.

Instantly three or four men close by opened fire in return, spraying the front of the shack. Ollie crouched low on the roof and turned his head anxiously. Lamar shouted for the shooting to stop but those who heard him right ignored him, and others thought he was calling on them to open fire. Ollie threw himself flat and angled his arm so that his pistol was pointing down through the gap in the roof but he had no chance of taking aim.

'Fool bastards!' Lamar sighted along his rifle, watching for movement at the door.

Anger burnt into Hart's face; now the thing had started up it wasn't going to finish until all the ammunition had been spent or whoever was inside the shack came tumbling out.

Fragments of wood spurted up from the logs alongside the windows, shells looped through the air as bullets winged their way aimlessly forward to bury themselves in the front of the building or ricochet harmlessly away. Ollie fired his pistol three times, twisting his arm round as far as he could to vary the angle. The noise was so great he had no way of knowing if he had hit any of the occupants or not. One of the ricochets whined close past his head and he pulled his head hard into his shoulders. Another spurted sod into his eyes and blinded him for several seconds. He knew that if he stayed where he was much longer his chances of getting off the roof alive were slim. He sent two more hasty shots down the chimney hole and thought he might have heard someone below roar with pain but he couldn't be certain. Hurriedly, he scrambled to the rear of the roof and jumped down into the narrow space between the back of the shack and the trees.

The front of the building seemed to shake under the onslaught of gunfire.

The door sagged back and was about to collapse.

Lamar squinted along the rifle and aimed at an arm which poked round one side of the door, attempting to set it to rights. His bearded face showed a moment's satisfaction as he saw the arm jerk and twist. More shots volleyed into the door and it tottered wildly, then sank backwards.

The shape of a man moved quickly through the space where the door had been and half a dozen bullets sought him out.

The sound of someone shouting from inside the shack pierced the racket of gunfire and excited shouting, but it was impossible to hear the words, to know if whoever it was was offering threat or submission. Both Hart and Lamar yelled for quiet, for a ceasefire, but it was no good.

'Jesus!' exclaimed Lamar. 'What a mess!'

The mess was made worse by one, then two more of the bounty hunters forsaking their positions and making a dash towards the besieged building.

Hart tightened his mouth and watched as one of them shuddered under a hail of fire from the cover of the shack. He seemed to be hit in the chest and belly, through both arms and in one of the legs. For seconds the force of the impact held him aloft, his body twisting as his face grimaced in pain. The other two hesitated, unmoving. As the dead man collapsed to the open ground, one of them decided to continue, the other attempted to regain the low ridge of land and safety.

Neither of them made it.

The one who ran back got within ten yards of his goal before a bullet drove through the back of his thigh and hurled him to the ground. Arm and head rolled and came up and as he pushed himself into a crouch another lucky bullet took the front of his skull away like it was paper caught in the wind. Skin and flesh flapped for a few urgent seconds, while blood and bone fragmented from beneath them.

Covering fire gave the third man the chance of making it to the shack. He zig-zagged most of the way, only sprinting straight when he was within close distance. He must have seen the open doorway like the end of his race for glory and a fat reward. Behind him shouts sang out as he leapt through the gaping space and swung his gun across the inside.

The stock of an empty rifle drove hard between his legs and made him trip, gasp and fall. Tears blinded his eyes and he fumbled with his pistol as the jarring landing sought to knock it from his hand. The rifle swung through a high arc and broke his forearm immediately below the elbow, the wooden stock splitting away from the metal of the rifle at the same time. The man screamed and pushed himself round with his other hand; he blinked his eyes open and through a pain-ridden blur saw a pistol thrusting towards his face. The gun exploded and the face was blown apart.

'What the hell's Ollie doin'?' said Lamar.

'Keepin' himself from gettin' killed,' answered Hart.

'Great!'

'What would you do?' Hart snapped back.

Lamar bristled. 'If that was me, I'd bust in there an' . . .'

'Get shot!' Hart finished for him.

Lamar didn't waste time arguing. He just glowered at Hart a moment or two and then fixed his attention back on the cabin. 'Those bastards've got it sewn up now. No one else is goin' to risk his life rushin' 'em and they can stay holed up in there for days, door or no door.'

'Unless they run out of shells.'

'Yeah,' agreed Lamar grudgingly. 'Or they maybe get bored with the scenery.'

Perhaps they did both. For whatever reason there was a sudden rush through the door, three men hurling themselves out that way and another two jumping through the windows. All five ran for the back of the place as fast as they could. It wasn't easy to figure out why, unless they thought they could make their escape through the trees and somehow leave the posse behind.

Maybe they had run down to their last few rounds of ammunition.

Maybe they couldn't take being cooped up there any longer.

Then again they could have been plain foolish.

Three of them went for the left side, two for the right. Those that went left ran into Ollie Halverton first. He was standing back of a couple of trees with his pistol resting over a low branch and he shot two of the men before they'd had time to figure out he was there. Lamar stopped one of the others from even getting past the front of the building by placing a slug from his Winchester plumb in the small of his back.

The rustler to have escaped Ollie's gun had little alternative but to try and make it back to the shack. It wasn't far to the door, but the window was closer. He hurled himself at the space, arms, head and chest diving through and his legs and behind waving in the air behind him.

Within seconds, they were riddled with bullets. The legs jerked hard enough to shake one of the boots almost off. They jerked some more and then they were still, blood and urine dripping down between them to the ground.

Disappointed to have missed him, Ollie moved to his left and intercepted the remaining man. For a split second they stared at one another in surprise. Both brought up their guns and fired and Ollie was the slower of the two. That didn't matter on account of he was the more accurate. A chunk of bark was clipped off an adjacent tree and sped away to the side. The man Ollie had shot clutched at his ribs, already feeling the blood begin to well through the torn skin, the sweat-stained and ridged clothing. His knees hammered down and he swallowed blood and bile and vomit, threatening to choke it back down his throat. His eyes were open but they could no longer see anything. Ollie thumbed back the hammer of the gun and watched, waited. The rest of the shooting seemed to have petered out. Men were running, shouting; he heard the voices of both Hart and Lamar above the rest. He watched as the wounded man's head jolted forward again and again, fingers splayed across his face and blood squirting through, brighter than it had any right to be. Bright and almost gleaming in the strong light of the sun. Ollie levelled his arm and squeezed deliberately back on the trigger.

They found branding equipment inside the shack, fitted up for half a dozen different brands. A bill of sale for a hundred head of cattle that almost certainly had not been theirs to sell. One of the men answered a description in the Rangers' *other* Bible close enough. One was a big man, bald head splattered with blood, eye patch torn from over a blind, purple-scarred socket. No one recognized him at all. The deputy swore that two of the others had been arrested for horse thieving six months back and managed to make their escape while they were being transferred from jail to court house. It might have been true and it might not. What was certain was that none of the men was John Wesley Hardin, nor looked remotely like him. When they were questioned, none of the posse could exactly recall who it was had first said that Hardin was amongst the bunch they were chasing.

Lamar eased the hefty dead man's body over with his boot so that the blind eye was no longer staring up at him. 'Reckon any of these could've been them as done for Lefty?'

Hart shrugged. 'Who knows?'

Lamar shook his head. 'I'd sure like to think so.'

The three of them walked back along to where their mounts were tethered. Ollie tried a little boasting of his own about how many men he'd put paid to, but it sounded too much like bragging about bringing down one-legged quail. Soon he shut up and their wasn't anything left to say. The place behind them stank of gunsmoke and loosed bowels and a lot of death.

None of them wanted to look back at the way the rest were dividing up the spoils, such as they were. Fingers cut off because rings refused to slip over swollen knuckles. Ears that would be sewn on to a length of rawhide and worn for good luck. A gold tooth hammered hard and brutally out of a mouth with the barrel end of a gun.

'Never did reckon Hardin was in there anyhow,' said Lamar.

The others glanced at him without replying.

A mile down the line, Ollie leaned over in the saddle and said to Hart: 'You think Hardin's still in the county?'

'He's got friends enough to keep him hid,' put in Lamar.

Hart shook his head. 'In the county,' he said, 'I wouldn't be surprised if he weren't in the the state.'

Ten

Alabama, winter 1876

The woman who counted the change into her purse, smiled briefly at the store keeper and lifted her purchases from the counter had once been a fine-looking creature. Would have been still if it hadn't been for the worn thinness of her face, the traces of tiredness under her eyes, the lines that etched themselves away from the corners of her mouth. Something, someone was wearing her out. Draining all the vitality from her.

The store keeper watched her, those thoughts running through his head, as she caught the young girl with her left hand, parcels swinging lightly from the right.

He'd seen it time enough – girls he'd watched growing up pretty as pictures, fresh as the blooms on a Black-Eyed Susan. One day they'd be flushed and excited on account of some man had asked to marry them and if not the next then soon enough afterwards, they began to change. The strain ate into them like woodworm into best oak. Oh, they survived it, most of them. If they noticed the change that had come over them he supposed they either reconciled themselves to it as inevitable or else found some way of blotting it out. But they survived because, by and large, they were stronger than men. There was a resilience there which kept them living, working, bearing children: a strength that was like steel inside them. Those that came to the frontier and stayed.

'Good day, Mrs Swain.'

She half-turned her head in the doorway and gave him a sense of a smile. Then the small bell rang as the door was closed and he could see her step off the sidewalk and deposit her things in the back of the carriage.

Her husband reached down from the driver's seat and lifted up the girl. Another child, younger, slept fitfully in a cot in the rear of the carriage. Mrs Swain leaned over it for a few moments before her husband called her to get in. The whip was already in his hand.

The store keeper thought about his own wife, his late wife, her memory slipping into his mind like the wind, keen and unbidden underneath the door. Fourteen years ago she had died giving birth to what would have been their first child.

'If I have to make a choice . . .?' the doctor had asked.

In the event it hadn't mattered; neither had survived.

He tried to think about something else, watched the carriage draw away and considered Mrs Swain's husband instead. On their regular trips to town this past four months, he had shown little of himself. Generally he seemed to have been content to let his wife do the marketing, waiting with the wagon or carriage, whichever they had driven. From time to time he would take a walk up to the livery stable and talk horse flesh with the owner there; occasionally he would stop in one of the main street saloons for a glass of whisky. Before he had sent for his wife it had been different. The visits to the saloon had been more frequent and had lasted longer. Swain had indulged what was clearly a strong interest in gambling; it was rumoured that on one or two occasions he had spent part of his winnings in one of the small rooms set back on the upper floor.

The store keeper was not surprised that Swain took his pleasures less openly since his wife had joined him. Vaguely he wondered where he took them now, but then since Swain travelled a good deal buying and selling cattle and horses there would be plenty of opportunities.

His final thought on the subject was whether his wife knew about his other interests and if so how much that contributed to the drawn expression which seemed now to be permanent on her face. At least, he consoled himself, he had remained faithful to his own wife while she had been alive – and, largely, since. A customer came in through the door and the bell jangled his head back to business.

'Put the child to bed.'

'She isn't tired now. She slept in the carriage driving back.'

'I said, put her to bed.'

'But, John . . .' She turned away from him, aware that arguing further was useless. More and more quickly they approached the point where words were no longer adequate for him and he had no alternative other than to show his frustration with blows. Once it had been enough to bang his fist on the table, strike the wall, the back of a chair. No longer. The first time he had struck her she had been too shocked to react; the second she had cried for the better part of an hour – not through pain, nor even fear. Rather a realization that this was what it had come down to and how it would remain. Why argue for what you want when you can get it with strength?

She picked up the little girl and carried her into the other room, settling her down close by the baby, wiping her mouth, her forehead, kissing her lightly on the cheek, whispering for her to hush and rest and later they would make the meal together.

'Jane!'

She sighed, straightened up, one hand to the small of her back. Her monthly had not come and it grieved her to think she might be with child again. She turned towards the door and his call, wondering why he insisted upon child after child when all they seemed to be most of the time for him was a nuisance. Something to be packed away from sight and kept quiet. Something to keep her occupied at home when he was away on business.

No – she glanced at her face in the mirror, pulled a few strands of hair into place – she doubted if he ever thought about it at all. It was simply natural to him; it was what married couples did; what wives were for – being mothers. Less and less did any of it have anything to do with pleasure.

'Jane!'

'I'm coming!'

Hardin was sitting in the deep rocker, tapping the slender fingers of his right hand against the polished wood of the arm. It caught at her – the realization that what had attracted her first about him had been his hands. The sight of them had stirred her inside the way nothing had before and little since. Mutual friends had described him long before they met. A brave young man, fighting against reconstruction and all that it stands for. She had wanted to meet him, this brave man. Brave and handsome. She had seen the slender hands, the handsome face with its fine moustache and she had believed the tales. Now she only knew that he liked excitement, courted it as once he had courted her. Gambling, horse racing, women, guns. She had slept alongside him only hours after he had emptied his pistol into a man's head.

'Tomorrow, I'm going to Florida. On business.'

Jane scarcely paused on her way to the stove.

'Didn't you hear what I said?'

'Of course.' She set one hand on the tea pot, swung her head. 'Don't you want some tea? My throat's dry after that ride.'

His hand came down on the chair arm with a loud slap and it rocked back violently as he stood up and started towards her. 'It don't mean a thing to you that I'm goin' away, is that it?'

'No, I . . .'

'Is it?'

'No!'

Instantly, she flinched at the sound of her own raised voice; watched and waited for his raised hand. Instead a smile curled about his mouth and when he next spoke his tone was soft and sarcastic.

'I expect you'll be glad to receive your callers.'

She fumbled with the pot, the top falling off with a small clatter. 'I don't know what you mean.'

'Of course you don't.' His eyes were smiling, but coldly, the way a man might look down on some animal he had trapped.

'John! What are you talking about – callers? I never . . .'

'No?' He was almost triumphant.

'You can't mean . . .?'

'Can't I?'

'Not that . . . that Ranger?'

Hardin slipped his hand down into his jacket pocket. From the next room came the sound of soft whimpering but it was soon fading again and lost in the crackle of the fire.

'How many times is it so far? Three or four?'

Tears pushed unbidden to the back of Jane's eyes. 'Two!' she almost shouted, spittle spraying from her lips. 'You know it was twice.' She turned her back to him. 'You know he came looking for you.'

'Sure. And found you. Both times.' Hardin paused long enough for her to think he was going to say nothing further before adding. 'Both times you told me about, that is.'

She screwed up her hands tight against her belly and at that moment wished more than anything else in the world that it was not a child she was carrying there. His child.

'You know I'm telling the truth,' she said, close to sobbing now and with her shoulders hunched away from him.

'Yes.' He set his fingers against her neck, under the dark ends of her hair and she shivered. 'I know. And I know I should have killed him when I had the chance.'

Jane shook her head and he moved his hand away. She stood there waiting for him to move away but, stubborn, enjoying her discomfort and fear, he remained close.

Jane had a picture of Hart then, clear in her mind. Tall and lean and angular, those faded blue eyes searching her through narrowed lids. She wondered if he had a woman, a wife. If he had children. She realized it was not the first time she had wondered these things.

'How long will you be away?' she asked, turning to face her husband.

Hardin shrugged. 'Week, ten days.'

'Selling stock?'

'Of course. I . . . don't cross-question me!'

She moved past him, taking the kettle towards the pump. 'I was just showing an interest. I thought that was what a good wife was supposed to do.'

Hardin wondered at the sharpness of her voice. It was unlike her to answer back in that way. He watched as she bent over the pump, her body framed by the door. He wanted to feel lust for her but could not; it had been a long time since he had and then only with the aid of too much whisky, too many thoughts of other women. Still, time enough when he was away . . .

'You will be back by Christmas?'

'Does it matter?' he asked, seeking to hurt her.

Jane stared at him a moment, then set the kettle on the stove. 'For the sake of the children,' she said.

Hardin nodded. 'I expect so. 'Less I get snowed up some place.'

'Shall you bring back a tree?' she asked a few moments later.

He didn't reply; perhaps he didn't hear her.

Jane touched her belly self-consciously and then went red for fear that he might have seen her. As soon as it was dark they would go to bed and unless he drank a great deal more he would roll on to his side, present her with his back and leave her alone apart from his light snoring. She knew that when he went off there were other women, whores from the dance halls and saloons he and his friends frequented. At first she had thought she could smell them on him when he returned, their cheap perfume and their used bodies, but it had been nothing more than her imagination. Now all she feared was that he should catch one of their diseases and bring it back to her.

Lying there, listening to her husband sleep, Jane Hardin smiled sourly at the thought that that might be the only present he would bring her home, this Christmas.

*

In the morning he was up and cleaning his guns before daybreak. She cooked his breakfast and roused the children, feeding them quietly, snatching glances at her husband now and then. He swallowed down a cup of coffee and started to the door.

'I'll be back as soon as I can,' he said briskly.

She could only just bring herself to look at him. Some of the baby's food dribbled back from his mouth and she wiped it on the edge of her apron.

'If your gentleman friend comes,' he began.

She looked at him then, her face fierce.

Hardin laughed, opening the door. 'Remember to give him my message.' And he slammed the door shut. Immediately both children began to cry. Jane Hardin held them to her and listened for the sound of the horse moving away, muffled soon by the snow that was beginning to fall. She wondered how wicked it was that part of her hoped against hope that he would never ride back.

Eleven

East Texas, spring 1877

Lamar's face was red with excitement, his voice beginning to show signs of hoarseness. The bottle close by was more than two-thirds empty. They'd been holed up in Galveston for three days already and it could be as long again before they got what they were after and were able to leave. If they ever got it. So much time sitting around waiting for something to happen, for a man to make a wrong move, for someone to see an opportunity for getting his revenge or making a wad of extra money. So many hands of five-card stud, so many yarns about women and horses and fights that became more and more elaborate with each retelling.

'. . . damn whale was the biggest I ever saw, bigger than you could imagine. I'm tellin' you, she comes towards the boat so fast and so damn huge she fair blocked out the sky. It was like one minute it had been the midst of day an' the next it was night and there you were with this small boat reelin' an' rockin' and the harpooner's hands tremblin' as he struggled to get the thing aimed right. We'd lost two men overboard and the whale was right upon us so close you could see its great jaw openin' and that minute the harpooner got swept clear out of the boat by this sudden wave.'

Lamar paused long enough to wipe the sweat from his face and take a quick swig at the bottle. Ollie Halverton leaned his thin body back against the thin hotel room wall and waited for the tale to reach its climax.

'There was nothin' else to be done. I pushed my way to the front of the boat and grabbed the harpoon, swingin' it up an' round. Just as the whale lunged its great ugly mouth towards the boat I . . .'

The board along the corridor creaked under a man's weight. Both Rangers sprang to their feet, pulling pistols free as they did so. Ollie slipped behind the door and Lamar put space between himself and the table.

The steps halted outside the door. It was a long couple of seconds before they heard Hart's voice. Both men released their breath slowly and Ollie reached forward and slid back the bolt. Hart came in briskly and took off his hat, skimming it across on to one of the narrow beds. His slicker was shiny black with rain. As he stood there water ran down on to the threadbare rug.

'Anything?' asked Lamar.

'Maybe.'

'You got a line on him?' asked Ollie.

Hart nodded and tugged the wet slicker over his head. He dropped it down close by the door. 'There's a cattle buyer name of Reardon,' he said. 'He's done business with a man goes by the name of Swain. J. W. Swain.'

'You reckon that's Hardin?' interrupted Ollie.

'Sounds a lot like him. Same appearance, claims to come from Alabama but sounds pure Texas. Wears a gun like he can use it and for all that he's successful, there's something about him that never quite relaxes. Like he's always expectin' to be jumped. Won't walk into a business meeting without having the place checked out first by one of the men who rides with him. Hardly ever travels without three or four men to back him up and although they're supposed to be partners in business, none of them ever says a whole lot. All they do is keep their eyes skinned and let it be seen they're well armed.'

Lamar offered the bottle to Hart, who shook his head and sat on the side of one of the beds.

'You show him a picture of Hardin?' asked Ollie.

'Yeah. He wasn't too certain when he saw it. But maybe he was gettin' a mite jumpy by then.'

'So what's next?' Lamar said.

Hart leaned back, taking his weight on his elbows. 'This Reardon, he's got a partner name of Caldicott. The pair of 'em have met up with Swain two or three times in the past few months, settin' up deals an' such. Cattle and horses. They've done a little gamblin' to pass the time. Swain, he takes his cards real serious.'

'That sounds right for Hardin,' put in Ollie.

Hart agreed. 'Caldicott's due in Galveston tomorrow unless anything happens to delay him. Reardon reckons he'll talk with us, take a look at the picture. If he says Swain and Hardin are the same man then it's pretty definite.'

'Except,' said Lamar, 'that in the last year we've had three others who were definite, too.'

'Yeah. Only this time I got a feelin' we're gettin' close.'

'Want him bad, don't you, Wes?' said Ollie.

Hart didn't reply right off, maybe didn't want to admit it. Finally he nodded and sat forward. 'He said how he was goin' to kill me, said it in front of witnesses. He ain't going to forget that an' neither am I. The longer he's running loose, the more time there is for us to meet up again and maybe next time he'll get the drop on me good. I don't want to risk that.'

'Hell! You ain't afraid of him? Just on account of he's got a reputation?'

Hart shook his head. 'I ain't afraid of no man face to face.'

Ollie broke the mood with a sudden laugh. 'Just like Lamar ain't feared of no whale. Not even one big enough to blot out the sun!'

Reardon and Caldicott were cautious men, especially when it came to talking to Texas Rangers who were acting outside their jurisdiction. They agreed to meet Hart in an eating house three blocks from the harbour on the condition that he went alone. Hart went along with the plan, but decided to use Lamar and Ollie as back-up just in case. He didn't think either of the two cattle buyers was about to set up a trap for him to walk into, but it wasn't out of the question for them to panic and refuse to talk. If that proved to be the case, Hart wasn't above using a little pressure and so having some men on hand to follow Reardon and Caldicott back to their hotels wasn't a bad idea.

The building was between a laundry and a dry-goods store, the street narrow and poorly lit. The wind was coming up from the south and Hart could smell the ocean as he dismounted and tethered his horse to the hitching rail. The place was a two-storey chop house with a long bar divided from a dozen tables on the ground floor by a heavy green curtain that hung from brass rings on a brass rail. The stairs were towards the rear at the right-hand side and led up to sixteen tables, half of which were in curtained booths.

Lamar won the toss of a coin with Ollie and got to sit up to the bar and swop lies with the bartender while he drank enough whisky to be a good customer and not so much that his reactions would begin to slow.

Ollie stationed himself out in the street, leaning against the side wall of a bakery, a couple of yards down into the alley. He hunched his narrow body into a wool coat and kept his head down, hat pulled hard on his ears. His hands were deep in his pockets and he was cursing the night for being cold and Lamar for winning the inside spot. He was certain that he'd been cheated but couldn't work out how.

Hart had deliberately arrived a little after the time of the meeting, wanting to come upon the two cattlemen already seated and settled. Not that either one of them looked composed as he came up to their central booth, concern clear on both faces. Reardon's face was florid as ever, the anxiety showing in his eyes and the way he never allowed the fingers of his hands to settle and be still. Caldicott was taller, more smartly dressed, a generous-sized cigar pushed into the side of his mouth. His cheeks were sucked in and close to chalk-white and when he shook Hart's hand the tremble was all too evident.

'You ordered?' Hart asked, sitting alongside Caldicott and opposite Reardon.

'Yes, we . . .'

'We didn't know . . .'

'That's okay.'

A waiter appeared and Hart surprised himself by ignoring the steaks and asking for a rack of lamb, potatoes and tomatoes. He joined the two men in a glass of beer. Reardon made a little small talk and his partner joined in with a few quiet remarks. Hart was mostly content to listen, in no hurry now that his informants were in place. Besides, he was hungry and sensed that if he brought the conversation to the point too hastily the meeting might break up before he could finish his meal.

The lamb, when it arrived, proved to be a good choice. Half a dozen linked chops, tender and juicy and almost sweet. Hart savoured them, amused at the lack of pleasure either of his dining companions were getting from their steaks.

At last, Hart leaned back and started his second glass of beer. Most of the other booths were full and the murmur of conversation stirred around them. He looked with some interest at a tall woman wearing a floor-length blue dress as she was escorted to a table opposite and allowed himself a half-smile. He refused one of Caldicott's cigars and rolled himself a cigarette.

When it was alight, he leaned forward again and said, 'Let's talk about Mister Swain.'

Caldicott gestured with his hand to suggest Hart had spoken too loud and Reardon shifted edgily on his seat. Hart reached into his pocket and pulled out an envelope; when he drew a wanted poster from within that and began to unfold it, he thought Caldicott might return his dinner to his empty plate right off.

'Don't you think,' began Reardon, 'a little more caution?'

Hart ignored him and held the flier in front of Caldicott's face, the likeness of John Wesley Hardin between the words of print. Caldicott blinked and the cigar bobbed up and down in his mouth. His face looked whiter than ever; it seemed to shine in the subdued light of the booth.

'Well?' Hart insisted after a few moments.

'I'm not . . .' Caldicott stuttered to a halt. He took the cigar from between his teeth and applied a match to the end even though it was still alight.

'Spit it out!'

Reardon leaned across the table and said: 'What do you think, Jed?'

Caldicott still looked like he was on the verge of bringing back his steak.

'You can read the figure at the bottom okay?' asked Hart with a sharper tone.

Caldicott nodded.

'Four thousand dollars,' Hart said, just in case.

Caldicott and Reardon exchanged glances and Hart could see the greed beginning to overcome their mutual fear.

'You're sure that we will be the, er, beneficiaries of this reward?' asked Reardon. 'I mean, we are taking a considerable risk here.'

Hart sat back. 'I ain't so sure about the risk. But as for the rest, you can see what it says – for information leading to the arrest of. You put our hands on Hardin and that four thousand dollars is yours.'

'But, Mister Hart,' began Reardon.

'Yeah?'

'If Swain and Hardin are one and the same, it does seem that he has turned his back upon Texas for good. And is leading a law-abiding life.'

'For the last time,' said Hart, 'that don't matter none. A couple of years dealin' in cattle don't wash away the past. And that's even allowin' for cattle dealin' bein' an honest profession.' Reardon gave him a hard look but he didn't feel strongly enough about it to speak out. 'As for not comin' back to Texas,' Hart went on, 'well, that's where his killin' was done and that's where he'll have to be tried. But if he won't come to Texas, then Texas'll have to come to him.'

'But surely you have no legal rights as law officers across the border?' asked Caldicott.

Hart grinned: 'I'm here now, ain't I? An' if we catch John Wesley Hardin fair an' square and get the drop on him, I don't see how any amount of legal hoo-ha's goin' to stop us from takin' him back to Texas.'

The two cattlemen exchanged more nervous glances; Hart decided it was time to push matters home. He allowed a movement of the tall woman's arm opposite to distract him momentarily and then thrust the flier at Caldicott again.

'Is that the man you been doin' business with as J.W. Swain or ain't it?'

Caldicott nodded and opened his mouth without speaking.

'Well?'

He nodded again.

'I want to hear it,' insisted Hart. 'Good and loud.'

'Yes,' agreed the man reluctantly. 'That's the same man. I'm . . . I'm . . . sure of it.'

Hart nodded, folded the poster and pushed it from sight. He sat back and glanced at both men. 'You deliver him to us and the money's yours.'

Caldicott dropped his cigar from his mouth; Reardon jerked his arm sharply and knocked a spoon clattering to the floor. The woman in blue glanced across at their table and Hart smiled at her but she swung her head back without acknowledging him.

'We understood—' Reardon finally spluttered.

'You understood what?' Hart snapped.

'That if we positively identified Swain as the man you were looking for then . . .'

Hart pointed a finger at Reardon and from the expression on the cattleman's face it might as well have been a gun. 'You want that reward, you're goin' to have to earn it better than that.'

'Keep your voice down, please,' said Caldicott, leaning across the table.

Hart ignored him; he knew he was doing well enough. 'We want to know where he's going to be on a particular day, a particular hour. We want that information an' you can give it to us.'

'The risk!' said Caldicott, fumbling with his cigar.

'There's no risk!' hissed Hart savagely. It was all he could do to stop himself from reaching across and grabbing Caldicott by the collar and shaking some sense into him forcibly. 'No risk at all.' He turned his attention back to Reardon. 'Here's what you do. Wait until there's a meeting arranged with Hardin, Swain, and let him make the plans as usual. Don't do a thing to make him suspicious. As soon as it's all set up, you let us know at Rangers' headquarters. We won't make a move until it's all over and you're both well clear. He'll be pleased the deal's gone through and more relaxed than before. That's when we'll take him.'

Hart stared at Reardon and waited for the man to reply.

When he didn't, Hart tapped the poster inside his pocket and said softly, 'Four thousand dollars. That's a lot of cattle.'

Reardon looked quickly at Caldicott and then nodded his head, sweat shaking from his red face and dripping on to the table. Hart could smell the fear on the pair of them and he knew that it was only the money that would prevent them from changing their minds after he'd gone. He wasn't positive that it was enough, but there was nothing else he could do.

'The information,' said Hart, already sliding out from the booth, 'you have it addressed care of Captain Armstrong. That understood?'

Reardon acknowledged that it was. Caldicott just stared in front of him, saying and doing nothing.

Hart straightened up. 'Thanks for the meal, gents. I trust we'll do business again some day.'

He turned on his heel and glanced at the woman in blue but she was intent on close conversation with her escort. He went smartly down the stairs and nodded towards Lamar at the bar. He was in the street and untying the reins of his mount when Lamar came out.

They walked together, leading their horses, to where Ollie was waiting.

'You took your time,' the thin man said grudgingly.

'The food was too good to rush,' said Hart with a grin.

'Whisky, too,' laughed Lamar.

Ollie cursed the pair of them roundly and they both laughed some more.

'Did you see that woman in blue who went upstairs?' asked Lamar as they turned out of the alley.

Hart nodded. 'Sure did.'

'She was something special, weren't she?'

'Uh-huh.'

'Jesus!' exclaimed Ollie. 'Were the pair of you tendin' to business or not?'

'Yeah,' replied Hart, slotting his boot into the stirrup and pulling himself up into the saddle, 'they reckon Swain's our man.'

'And they'll play along with the rest?'

Hart shrugged. 'They say they will. It depends how far off it is and how greedy they are at the time.'

'What're the chances?' asked Lamar as they rode down the narrow street.

'I'm not sure. But if I were a betting man, I don't think I'd like the odds.'

'Never mind,' said Ollie, 'Hardin's the bettin' man, not you. Let's hope this time he don't know every card in the deck.'

The long ride home was uneventful, aside from Hart's horse

throwing a shoe and Lamar managing to clean the others almost out of what little money they had left. He celebrated by stopping at a way station and buying a bottle of good whisky which he shared willingly, recounting at the same time the yarn he'd told half a dozen times before about how during the War Between the States, he infiltrated the Pinkertons while working as a secret agent for the Confederacy. Hart couldn't help but notice how this time the woman he seduced in order to carry out his plan was wearing a long blue evening dress at the time. Well, part of the time.

Himself, he tried to stop thinking about the way it had finished between himself and Kathy; he thought some about Hardin's wife, Jane, instead, but that didn't seem to work. The only thing that did was Lamar's whisky which numbed the hurt away the same as it did for an aching tooth.

The one matter they all thought about but didn't discuss was their informants. Each mile further on they rode, the chances of Reardon and Caldicott coming through seemed weaker and weaker, as if in taking on a new name Hardin had succeeded in setting himself beyond their reach.

Twelve

August 1877

Spring had warmed into summer and no message had come from either Reardon or Caldicott. The Rangers had become immersed in other things. If Hardin had made up his mind to stay out of the state and out of reach, maybe there was little they could do about it. Still it riled Hart mightily that he was off somewhere in Alabama living the life of a married man with kids and a regular home, all that with so many killings to his credit while Hart himself had finally got nothing from the woman he loved but the image of her head turning away and her last words fading into the wind. Kathy. There were times when the thought of her – of knowing her and not being able to have her – threatened to break him. And at those times when he wanted to get off on his own, the outfit's regulations made such an action impossible. So Hart itched with all manner of frustrations that summer of seventy-seven. Frustrations which weren't eased by what took place in Marshall that July.

Captain Armstrong had detailed him to go over there, along with Ollie Halverton, Lamar and Keogh. They found themselves in the middle of a long-running conflict between the Texas and Pacific Railroad and its workers about wages and conditions. A new union, the Trainmen's Union, was having a lot of success all over the country in pushing a hard line and there'd been strikes and walkouts and, in quite a few places, violence had flared with troops being ordered in and blood being shed. The Trainmen sent down a feller called Ira Davis to stir things up; he had a spotted kerchief in his vest pocket, a briefcase packed with facts and figures and a gimpy leg from where he had an accident working as a brakeman. And he could talk!

Needless to say, the Texas and Pacific wanted Hart and the other Rangers to ride in and drive Davis back where he came from, break up any possible strike and force the men back to work. But it wasn't as straightforward as that. For one thing the Rangers weren't on the railroad payroll and for another it seemed as if them as were had maybe been getting a raw deal for long enough. In the end the four Rangers were stuck in the middle with very little they could do other than try to make sure not too many innocent folk got hurt. It was a bloody mess, right enough, but maybe not as bloody as if they'd not been there at all.

At the end of the month the Texas and Pacific forked out the back pay the strikers were demanding and promised that a raise in wages would be recommended. Hart had shrugged when he'd heard the news; from what he'd seen of the railroad officials, recommended was about as far as it would go.

The whole thing did little to make Wes Hart happier with life as a Texas Ranger. He was feeling the need for space and distance, for his own way of life, his own company. He was thinking vaguely along those lines, doing some hankering after the plains of Montana, when Keogh's round face showed round the bunkhouse door.

'Busy?'

'Not so's anyone would notice.'

'Captain wants you.'

The letter was open on the captain's desk, small, well-formed words that Hart could not read upside down. He waited to be asked to sit down, did so looking at the smile that wasn't quite making its appearance on Armstrong's leathered face.

'Son . . .'

'Yeah.'

'They finally did it. They come through.'

Still Hart wasn't sure. He watched the smile emerge and then he thought he was. 'Reardon and Caldicott.'

Armstrong nodded, laughed, lifted up his cane and brought it back down on to the corner of the desk with a resounding slap. 'Either you put the fear of God into 'em or they want them dollars real bad or both, but if what they say here's true, we could have our chance.'

He used the tip of the cane to push the letter across the desk towards Hart, who took it up and turned it around and read it. Twice.

'Well?' asked Armstrong with maybe a sign of impatience. 'Ain't that what we been waitin' for?'

Hart still wasn't certain.

'Hell, son! I don't know what you was expectin' from these fellers? Hardin's head on a silver platter?'

Hart shook his head. 'Pensacola ain't Texas,' he said.

'That what's worryin' you?'

'It's one thing.'

Armstrong pointed the cane at Hart and winked broadly. 'May not be Texas, but it's sure as hell close enough.'

Hart glanced at the letter again and dropped it down on to the desk.

'I reckoned,' said Armstrong, drawing out his words, 'as you'd be a sight more pleased.'

Hart hesitated. 'So did I.'

Armstrong nodded, folded the letter. 'Somethin's eatin' into your craw, Wes, ain't it?'

Hart looked at him, saying, doing nothing.

'You want to talk about it?'

'Uh-uh.'

The captain nodded again, more curtly this time. 'Okay. That's your privilege, I guess. Only . . .'

'Only what?'

'Just don't let it get in the way of what you're about.'

'I won't.' There was anger straining at the edges of Hart's voice and his eyes had narrowed the way they did when he was facing a man whose gun he was going to have to take away. Except that it wasn't so easy to take away words.

'Man here,' said Armstrong, 'he's a Ranger first an' other things second.'

'I know that.'

The captain pressed both hands on to the edge of the desk hard. 'All right. First time you don't, you know what you got to do.'

'Don't worry,' said Hart, getting to his feet. 'Any time I don't think I can do the job any more I'll tell you before you get the chance to tell me.'

Armstrong shook his head. 'Hell, son, you can do the job. You're . . .' He stopped and watched Hart turn towards the door. 'Want him bad, don't you? Hardin, I mean.'

Hart turned slowly. 'I guess.'

'I never asked you your reasons.'

'Maybe I never figured 'em out.'

'He did threaten to kill you. That'd be enough for most men.'

Hart nodded: 'Maybe it is.'

'Sure,' agreed Armstrong. 'Except that it isn't.' He swung his cane to the floor and used it to lever himself up. There were good days for his leg and bad days and this one was a horned bitch. He stared at Hart keenly, weighing what he was going to say. 'It ain't nothin' to do with that wife of his? You ain't got the hots for her or anything, have you? I mean, the two of you ain't carryin' on?'

It seemed so absurd to Hart that he blurted out a laugh. 'For God's sake! You and Hardin both.' It only occurred to him later how close Armstrong was edging up on the truth, though not in the same was as he'd meant it. 'I saw her twice, that's all. Questioned her about Hardin. Routine.'

Armstrong nodded. 'He figured it for somethin' more.'

'Then he's a jealous fool.'

'Sure.' He rapped his cane. 'Okay, son. We'll run this through in a day or so, make sure we've got it sewed up tight. We ain't goin' to get but the one chance.'

When Hart left the office, Armstrong poured himself a shot of rye and lit a stumpy cigar and wondered what had happened to that pretty woman Hart had been passing time with. He wondered if she was what was the burr under his saddle and hoped that she wasn't. Either way, he figured she was one more reason why when they went across the state line for Hardin, Wes Hart was going to be well back in the shadows.

The meeting with Reardon and Caldicott was set for the twenty-second. They'd hired a private room in the State Hotel in Pensacola and business was to be brought to a satisfactory conclusion over duck and cherry sauce and the obligatory bottle of champagne. John Wesley Hardin – or J.W. Swain – never seemed properly happy unless a business deal was crowned with champagne. Once the celebrations were over, Hardin and whoever had accompanied him would board the train at Pensacola junction and return to Alabama.

Armstrong had given the Florida cattlemen his word that no move would be made against the fugitive while he was at the State Hotel, nor at any time when the two informants were likely to be endangered.

'The train,' the Rangers captain said. 'We'll take him when he's on the train. We'll take him before it pulls out of the station. He'll be in a confined space and won't be able to run. Chances are the drinkin' won't have left him any too sharp. For certain, he won't be expectin' trouble.' Armstrong gave it his good smile. 'I think we got him good!'

The plan was simple enough. The Texas Rangers would wait at the rail station, out of sight. As soon as Hardin and his party boarded the train, a man would move in to seal off both exits to the car. Then Captain Armstrong himself, with two men as back-up, would climb on board and confront Hardin. If he agreed to go quietly, so much the better. If not . . .

'He ain't never gone quiet before,' said Keogh.

'I ain't never arrested him before,' laughed Armstrong.

The others laughed too, but then as the amusement faded, Lamar said, 'These two goin' into the coach with you, how 'bout slippin' one of 'em round the other side, let him come in the other door?'

'You volunteerin'?' smiled the captain.

Lamar raised an eyebrow. 'Why not?'

'Okay. You got the job. Just make sure you don't get glory-crazy and set foot in the coach too soon.'

Lamar nodded, thinking that none of them was going to be able to steal any glory from the captain on this trip – whatever was to be had from taking John Wesley Hardin prisoner, Armstrong wanted it all.

'Your back-up,' said Hart, leaning forward, 'you got any one of us staked out for that?'

Armstrong knew what was coming. Still he said, 'Why, Wes?'

'I'm volunteerin'.'

Armstrong shook his head slowly. 'An' I'm turnin' you down.'

Hart's stomach tightened. 'How come?' The words came a little too fast, a little too angry from his mouth.

Armstrong tightened his grip on the top of his cane and let Hart see that he'd overstepped the invisible line. 'Son, I'd as soon have you back of me as any man I've served with. Sooner than most. But Hardin knows you by sight and he's swore to get you on a personal matter. Leastways, it's personal as he sees it. One glimpse of you an' his temper's goin' to be up in his throat and he's more likely to make a play for his gun whatever else.' He paused, watching Hart's face. 'No, I want you out of line, out of sight. I want you on the platform guardin' the rear entrance to that car. You're there an' I know it's sewn up and there ain't nobody bustin' out. That'll make me feel good.'

Hart didn't like it; he didn't like what Armstrong had told him and neither did he appreciate the way the others, Keogh, Ollie, Lamar and the rest, were looking at him, waiting for him to react. He bit down on his anger and gave a curt nod. 'Sure,' he said. 'That's fine.'

'Okay.' Armstrong looked around at the men. 'Ollie, I been hearin' good things 'bout you lately. I want you steppin' into the coach right back of me.'

Ollie blushed and scratched his ear and went redder still and tried not to sound too proud when he agreed. Armstrong gave out the rest of the assignments. Keogh was to watch the opposite end of the car to Hart and a Ranger by the name of O'Reilly would be back down the platform just in case things went badly wrong and one of Hardin's men managed to break clear.

'When's it to be?' asked Lamar.

'Train's due out at thirty minutes after nine tonight. Hardin's meeting up with Reardon and Caldicott at five. The private room's booked till a quarter after nine.'

'Do we know how many he'll have with him?' asked Keogh.

'Reardon reckons not more than three. Twice before he's had that number, once just two. But it ain't them we're concerned with. John Wesley Hardin's all we want. You remember that.' He looked sternly around his men. 'All of you.'

*

The station building was forty feet long and partitioned into three, the central section being the ticket office and the main entrance from the street. To one side was a small dining room with four square tables and a broad stove which was giving out a sight too much heat for a warm night. The other side was mostly used as a freight depot for the various goods the line handled. It was in here that Captain Armstrong waited, along with Ollie Halverton and Lamar. Lamar was well into one of his tall tales but no one was listening, least of all the captain, who prodded around between the crates and trunks as if moving was the only thing that kept his heart pumping blood. He leaned heavily on his cane, keeling over towards the left; his leg was giving him merry hell and he didn't know for sure if that was a true sign that Hardin was on his way or not. Occasionally he would stop his rambling and lash out with the cane, thwacking it against some heavy object as if it were the gunman's face. Lamar hardly paused in his yarn. Ollie leaned against a wicker box and tried to pretend that his guts were not churning over fit to make butter and cream both.

Keogh and O'Reilly sat in the stifling heat of the diner and slowly drank warm beer. Hart stood back across the tracks, deep in the shadow of a couple of unused cattle trucks. The Alabama train was standing thirty yards short of the platform, all serviced and fuelled and ready to shunt forward and pick up the passengers who were waiting to begin their journey.

Fourteen passengers and none of them John Wesley Hardin.

'What in hell's name's gone wrong?' demanded Armstrong, fetching a tin box a tremendous clout with his cane. 'Where is he?'

Neither Lamar nor Ollie had an answer. Lamar hesitated a few moments before launching back into his story but was no more than a dozen words in before Armstrong turned on him and told him to shut up and let him think.

Lamar scowled and pushed his fingers through his thick beard; Ollie turned his head aside so that Lamar wouldn't see him smiling. Even then, it was the first thing he'd had to smile about for a long time.

Wes Hart stood with a cigarette cupped tight between the fingers of his left hand, the palm of the right resting on the pearl-handled grip of his Colt .45. Hardin wasn't going to show. He knew it in his belly and he'd known it for the past half-hour. He didn't know why but he was positive his feelings were right. With half a mind to cross over the track and tell Armstrong, he held back. He was as likely to get bawled out for quitting his position as thanked – and there was always the possibility that he was wrong. Hardin could still come.

With a slow rumble of steam, the engine came forward on to the track alongside the platform. The two Rangers left the diner and stretched their legs, watching the boarding passengers carefully. None of them could possibly have been Hardin, not even had he taken it into his head to disguise himself against discovery.

Armstrong rubbed at the dirty glass and peered out. Although it was yet light, the kerosene lanterns that overhung the platform had been put to use. He scanned left and right, cursed, and repeated the process in the opposite direction. With another curse he growled at Ollie to fetch Wes Hart as soon as the train pulled out.

'You don't reckon Hardin's goin' to show?' asked Ollie and earned himself a place in the captain's personal perdition.

Fifteen minutes later the train drew out of the station with much clatter and steam and before its iron rumble receded, the red rear lights easily visible, Hart had joined Armstrong in the freight depot.

'What's your guess?' snapped Armstrong.

'That he's got drunk, got into a game of stud, found a woman – maybe all three.'

'Yeah,' the captain agreed. 'It rings true.'

'You want me to go into town an' check?'

Armstrong nodded. 'Yeah. There's the risk of you bumping into Hardin, but if what you reckon is correct, that ain't so likely. Not if you play it safe. Wait an hour or so, then slip in. Forget about looking for Hardin direct. Concentrate on Reardon. He knows you and that's better than facing him with one of us an' scarin' him into warning Hardin off. Find Reardon and see what's happened for sure. When Hardin's plannin' on makin' his move. Report back to me here.'

'Okay,' said Hart and turned to go.

'Lamar,' said Armstrong, 'you're always claimin' to have been some kind of undercover detective. You tag along with Wes, keep in his shadow, don't scare Reardon into running. You understand?'

Lamar acknowledged that he did; he followed Hart out through the door and along the now-deserted platform.

The bar wasn't big enough to knock a man down and expect him to fall flat. It was thick with smoke and stank of lamp oil and cheap liquor. The price of a shot of whisky or tequila was lower than anywhere else in Pensacola, which was why the place was so crowded. Hart elbowed his way through to the bar and ordered a whisky and right off he discovered why it was so cheap. But then he wasn't there to enjoy a drink.

The girl had been pointed out to him as she crossed the narrow street, a shiny silk scarf tied tight about her bare neck, one end of it draped across her bare shoulders. She was one part Mexican, one part Apache and the rest white. Her eyes were dark and spiteful and she had the second most beautiful mouth that Hart had seen in a long time. She pursed it in his direction as he squeezed his way towards her.

'Hello!' She smiled up at Hart and he knew that behind the smile she was estimating how much money he might have in his wallet and how much she would have to do to get it from him. He didn't think any the worse of her for that.

He leaned over and tried to avoid looking down the front of her dress. She smiled and adjusted her position so that he couldn't but do anything else.

'You want something?' she asked, certain that she knew the answer.

'Sure.' He pulled a greenback from his pants pocket and held it before her. 'You were in the State Hotel earlier. Private room.' Her eyes were already glinting and she showed him the length of the nails on her right hand. 'It's okay,' Hart hastened to reassure her, 'I don't want trouble. Least of all for you.'

'What then?'

'Information.'

She studied his face, then the note; slowly she took it from between his fingers and transferred it to the top of her dress. She held out her hand for more. Hart ignored her gesture and said: 'A man called Swain was there?'

She didn't move her hand but kept it open; she kept her beautiful mouth shut.

Hart carefully closed the fingers of her hand.

'Swain,' he repeated.

'Yes,' she said.

'Describe him to me.'

She did.

'Okay. There were two men with him called Reardon and Caldicott.'

The fingers unravelled themselves; Hart filled them with another bill.

'Yes,' she said.

'They paid you to be there?'

She nodded.

'What happened when it all broke up? Where did they go?'

'The three you mentioned?'

Hart nodded yes.

'Caldicott, he was drunk. He'd been moaning about having a headache all evening. He went back to his room at the hotel.'

'The same hotel?'

'Of course.'

'And Swain?'

A trace of anger came to her face and her voice became thicker. 'He wanted to gamble. The others, they kept telling him he had a train to catch, they made jokes about going home to his wife. He told them there was always another train. He paid two of the girls to go to a poker game with him and his friends. Then to where he was staying.'

'The same place?'

She shook her head. 'I don't know. I don't think so.'

He offered her a third bill.

She took it but she still didn't know which was Hardin's hotel, except she had understood it was not the State.

'Okay,' said Hart, 'tell me about Reardon. Where is he now?'

'I think he was going to eat in the hotel, then go to bed.'

'Alone?'

'Unless he finds someone else there.'

'None of the women stayed with him?'

She shook her head. Her eyes were looking more than a little tired, more than a little worried; her mouth looked as good as ever. Hart wondered what the other two girls had looked like that Hardin had chosen to pay for their company rather than hers. Then he remembered the stories about the gunman's hatred of anyone who wasn't white.

He didn't need to give her any more money but he did. 'Get yourself a drink,' he said. 'And don't tell anybody you've been talking to me or what about.' It wasn't his money he was spending. The grudging smile she gave him as he shouldered his way back through the crowd suggested that she knew that only too well.

Outside, Hart picked up Lamar and told him to go over to the State Hotel and check which room Reardon was staying in. When he knew the answer, he went round to the back stairs and told Lamar to keep watch.

Thirteen

The top of the window was open by little more than an inch to let in the warm night air. The sounds of the town had more or less faded to a murmur of voices, the occasional discordant laugh. The window frame squeaked in its casing. Hart held his breath. Waited. Tried again. Again it squeaked, refused to budge, wobbled, finally yielded. He bent low and eased his way over the sill and between the flimsy curtains.

The shape in the bed stirred and changed position, settled once more. Hart went quietly close, set one hand poised over Reardon's mouth and with the other prepared to shake him awake.

The cattleman twisted and bucked and tried to shout but the pressure of the sweaty fingers over his mouth was too great. His head wanted to throw itself sideways but couldn't; his frightened eyes swivelled and even in the vague light recognized Hart.

Reardon's fear kicked him hard in the belly.

'It's okay,' Hart said, keeping his voice low. 'Ain't nothin' goin' to happen to you.'

Reardon looked far from convinced.

'I just want to talk. Nothin' more.'

Reardon tried to move and Hart released the pressure of his hands sufficiently to allow the cattleman to straighten on to his back but no more.

'You give me your word you ain't goin' to shout out, I'll take this hand off'n your mouth.'

Reardon tried to nod.

'I got your word?'

The head moved slightly; the eyes said he had.

Hart slowly slid his hand away and straightened his back. The room smelt of sweat and the aftermath of an evening's heavy drinking. Reardon pushed himself up into a sitting position in the bed, his breathing rough and uncertain.

'He didn't come for the train,' Hart said flatly.

'That weren't our fault.'

'Didn't say it was.'

'He got more'n half-way drunk and feelin' randy and someone said something about a big poker game.' Reardon shook his head. 'That boy does love his gambling.'

'You sure that's where he went?'

'Yes. He took a couple of girls and said he was going to double what he'd just made in our deal. Made one of the men with him go and order rooms at the Palace.'

Hart nodded; he'd noticed the hotel down the street as they'd come from the station. 'There's no way he could've changed his mind and hired horses and ridden out?'

'The way he was feelin'? He'd've fallen off his horse for sure unless they'd roped him on.' Reardon shifted in the bed, plumping the pillow up behind him. 'Besides, he wasn't quitting that game. Or them two women.'

'What are his plans, Reardon?'

'There's a train tomorrow night. Not so direct, he'll have to break his journey, but it's that or a three-day wait.'

'Maybe he'll do that?' suggested Hart, thinking how difficult it would be for the Rangers to remain under cover and out of Hardin's way for that length of time.

But Reardon was shaking his head. 'He sent someone down to the station to change the tickets. Said something about other business.' An idea caught at the back of Reardon's mind and he couldn't shake it. It showed in his face.

'What is it?' Hart asked.

'You ain't going to wait, are you? You're going to take him here in town. At this hotel.'

Hart shook his head. He'd been thinking the very same thing himself and as an idea it had a lot to commend it. Especially if Hardin was getting over a hangover and his reactions would be dulled. But lawmen had tried to get the drop on him in town before and each time there'd been enough extra guns around for him to fight his way out. Besides, drunk or sober, he expected trouble in town. Hart was positive he did so even now that he was J.W. Swain and he was a successful businessman. He guessed that Hardin was always ready in hotel rooms and bars, however drunk he might seem to those around him. And in town there were too many possibilities of escape.

'No,' he said, 'we're stickin' to our plan. Just as long as he is. We'll take him on the train.'

Reardon nodded, wiped his head, reached towards the glass of water beside his bed.

'Two more things,' said Hart.

'Go ahead.'

'How many men with him, two or three?'

'Four.'

Hart repeated the number aloud. It was one more than they'd reckoned on and it might mean that Hardin was feeling suspicious and expecting some kind of trouble.

'Names?' he said.

'There's a young feller called Mann. Jim Mann. Don't look a lot more than a boy. Daley Carson, he's been with him before. The other two were called Mason and Masters, something close to that.'

None of the names meant anything to Hart. 'Where was he wearing his gun?' he asked.

Reardon had to think.

'You must have . . .'

'He wasn't wearing a gun-belt, I'm sure of that. No. No, I didn't see a weapon, unless . . .'

'Unless what?'

'The whole evening, he didn't take off his coat.'

'A shoulder holster, then?'

'It's possible. I couldn't swear to it, but, yes, it's possible.'

Hart nodded. 'How 'bout the others?'

'The youngster, he was wearing a gun tied to his leg. I'm certain of that. Shiny leather holster like he'd bought it here in town. Carson the same, almost for sure. I think Mason and Masters weren't armed.'

'All right.' He pointed a finger at Reardon. 'When are you leaving town?'

'First thing. Well, after breakfast. Caldicott and I are meeting in the dining room and then we're set to leave. Don't you worry about that.'

Hart was worrying about quite a few things, but that wasn't one of them. He warned Reardon to keep his mouth closed, even to his partner, and left the room the same way he'd entered.

Lamar was waiting below. 'He's still here, ain't he?'

Hart nodded.

'Why don't we take him? I mean now. You an' me. We could do it.'

Hart shook his head. 'Maybe we could. That ain't the point.'

'No?' Lamar stopped him. 'What is?'

Hart made to go round him, but the bearded man thrust himself in the way. 'You realize what it'd mean? If we took John Wesley Hardin?'

Hart set a hand on Lamar's shoulder. 'If we tried and struck lucky – an' that's a hell of a big if – the only thing it'd mean would be a reputation. The man who took John Wesley Hardin. You want to live with that? Think about it, Lamar. You'd be the target for every young punk out to make a name for himself. Every drunk who thinks he's the fastest gun in town. Besides . . .' he tightened his grip on the man's arm '. . . you've already got enough to brag about.'

Lamar shrugged Hart's hand away. There was a lot of sense in what Hart said and he knew it without wanting to admit that it was true. Added to which they both knew that Captain Armstrong was determined to make the arrest himself. He hadn't left his desk and dragged his bad leg all the way to Florida to sit back while two of his men stepped out of line and took his prize away from him.

The two men went back to the station and told Armstrong what they knew. He sent Keogh in to confirm that a Mister Swain was registered at the Palace Hotel. Then he paid a visit to the station master and arranged that as far as possible the coach Hardin was boarding would be clear of other passengers. After that it was just a matter of waiting.

Hardin had dinner in the hotel and settled down to play a few hands of five-card stud before it was time to stroll down the street towards the station. His headache and the ache in his gut had both left him and he was in good humour. Even dropping thirty dollars to young Jimmy Mann didn't upset him too much. Mann played cards the way he did everything – fast and anxious. Hands reached out and grabbed the cards before they hit the table, his bid was out of his mouth before everyone else had sorted their deal. The expression of excitement that so readily came to his face didn't give anything away. Jim Mann was capable of getting excited about a pair of threes and nothing else.

'You want Masters an' me to walk down the station, check things out?' asked Mason edgily.

'What the hell for?' demanded Hardin. 'Case someone's stolen the train?'

Jim Mann laughed; Mason didn't. He was as nervous as a cat on heat.

'What's eatin' you?' Hardin asked, not appreciating anyone else being worried when he was feeling good.

Mason shrugged, sat down, stood up again, walked around the table.

'Go and get yourself a drink. Get laid. Do something to steady them nerves of yours. Anyone'd think you ain't never ridden a train before.'

'That's the trouble,' Jimmy Mann offered, 'he didn't get laid last night.'

'And you did, I suppose?' retorted Mason, rubbing his hands together.

'You bet!' called Mann and dropped one of his cards. He'd been the only one of them to have slept alone and he guessed they knew it.

'Never mind, kid,' said Hardin, pushing the bottle in his direction. 'You concentrate on this hand. I got about fifteen minutes to win that money back.'

'All right,' said Armstrong, 'let's go over it one last time.'

The men gathered inside the freight depot looked and listened. It was half an hour before the train was due to pull out.

'Wes, you and Keogh take an end of the car each. You seal it off as soon as Hardin and his party are on board. Any other passengers try to get on, you steer 'em well clear. And watch out for anyone trying to get off. Lamar, when you've seen Ollie an' me make our move towards the coach, give us time to get on and then get yourself in from the other end. Make it fast, make it quiet and don't make it too soon.'

Lamar nodded, shifted his weight on to his other foot.

'O'Reilly, you stay by this door, watch the platform. Anyone manages to get past Wes and Keogh and they don't get past you. That understood?'

It was.

'Questions?'

'What if a couple of the men with him hang back? Around the diner or something.' It was Hart's question.

'Use your judgement. If they look as if they're goin' to hold off for some time, then we'll go ahead and you'll have to watch both ways. If it starts to look difficult, signal to O'Reilly for help.'

Hart seemed satisfied. No one else had any questions. Captain Armstrong checked his watch. 'Let's get to our positions,' he said.

Hardin was wearing a dark three-piece suit with a short-brimmed hat and black boots inside his pants. He carried a small case under his left arm. His .44 was in a holster attached to his suspenders, the butt almost poking out from the lapel of his jacket. Before leaving the hotel he'd automatically checked the load and spun the chamber.

'Expectin' trouble?' asked Mason, whose jumpiness had failed to subside.

Hardin shook his handsome head. 'No,' he answered. 'An' neither should you be. Why don't you relax and enjoy the trip? We can play a few hands as we pull out.'

Jim Mann grinned and vowed how he was going to take them all for every cent they had. All five men were still laughing about that when they entered the station. They walked past the booking office and out on to the centre of the platform. The train had pulled in some ten minutes before. Daley Carson pointed along to the small diner. 'Shall I get a bottle?' he asked.

'I already got a bottle,' said Masters.

'Me too,' said Hardin.

Carson still hesitated. 'I guess I'll get another. We got a long journey.'

'Okay,' agreed Hardin, starting to move towards the train. 'Only hurry it up, we don't want to leave without you.'

'Yeah,' called Jim Mann, 'nor your money, neither.'

Daley Carson shook his head and went off to get his bottle of whisky. The other four men wandered along the platform and the station master stepped over and intercepted them.

'Mister Swain, sir?'

'What is it?' Hardin broke his stride.

'There's a coach up towards the engine for you and your party, sir. You can have a little privacy up there. As far as your next stop, anyway.'

Hardin looked at the man's beady eyes peering out from beneath the peak of his uniform cap. The light from the kerosene lantern hanging overhead cast sharp shadows on the boards.

'Okay,' said Hardin, 'you show us the way.'

The railroad man walked ten yards and stopped by the couplings between two coaches. 'Here you are, Mister Swain.'

Hardin nodded and sent Masters and Mason ahead. Mason called out that it was okay to board, but Hardin was already on the iron steps.

'I hope you'll travel with us again, sir,' said the station master, trying not to back away too quickly.

Hardin swung his head, ignoring the man in uniform and looking back along the platform for Carson. Between himself and the diner, a man and woman were sauntering alongside the train; another man, wearing a white suit and hat, was climbing on board lower down. There was a pile of freight waiting to be loaded.

'Jimmy,' said Hardin, 'go hurry that fool on.'

'You bet!'

But Hardin called out after the youth when he was no more than a couple of paces away. 'Forget it! Let him take his own time. It's this damn Mason gettin' me in a sweat. Come back and get settled. Carson'll be here with time a-plenty.'

Jim Mann shrugged and did as he was told. He didn't see why Daley Carson had needed to go off for yet more whisky anyhow. But then he didn't consume nearly as much as the rest of them.

Wes Hart saw one of Hardin's men start off down the platform, looking as if he was going in search of the one already in the diner. Then he heard a voice he presumed to be Hardin's, though he couldn't distinguish the words, and saw the man turn back on his heels and board the train.

Why the hell hadn't they all boarded together?

He looked out for a sign that the captain was making his own move, but he appeared to be giving Hardin time to relax and settle down. Back along the platform there was no sign of the fifth man emerging. Hart smoothed his palm along the butt of his Colt, mouth tight shut, nerves honed to the sharpest edge. His stomach was flat and hollow. The door to the diner opened and someone came out. Hart wedged himself deeper back into the shadow and watched as the man boarded the train lower down. It could have been the one he was looking for but it wasn't light enough to be sure. He might have got on the train at the nearest point and be intending to walk through from car to car until he found Hardin.

Hart hesitated, uncertain what to do.

In the midst of that uncertainty, Captain Armstrong nudged Ollie Halverton and made his move from the door of the freight depot to the train.

Inside the coach Hardin took off his hat and flicked it neatly on to one of the empty seats. He flopped down into the seat nearest to him, the springs complaining so loudly that a couple of the men laughed and Jimmy Mann threw out a remark about Hardin's weight. Mann promptly sat facing him on the opposite side of the aisle. Mason hesitated about sitting facing the engine or not and finally chose the window seat next to Hardin. That left Masters in the aisle.

He was still there when Captain Armstrong clambered up

the steps and threw back the coach door. The only one facing him was Jimmy Mann and nothing about the Ranger seemed to register. Armstrong was using a cane and although he had a holster tied down to his right leg, his gun was safe inside it.

Masters turned his head at the noise and said, 'This coach is private.'

Armstrong grunted something inaudible and took a couple of clumsy paces along the gangway.

'I said . . .'

But now there was another man close behind the first and things didn't look so good. Hardin saw doubt flicker across Masters' face and he pushed himself up and round in his seat. He didn't need to recognize Armstrong to understand.

'Texas, by God!' he shouted and twisted the top half of his body, hand plunging inside his coat. Jimmy Mann let out a nervous laugh and sprang to his feet. The door at the far end of the coach opened with a slam and Lamar cannoned into Masters' back. The pair of them fell sideways, half on to and half off the seats, struggling and punching.

Hardin's fingers tightened on the butt of his .44 and he jerked it from the holster. Half-way clear, the foresight snagged against the elastic of his suspender.

Jimmy Mann thumbed back the hammer of his Smith and Wesson and fired from just above the hip, the shell skimming through the crown of Captain Armstrong's hat.

Armstrong straightened his right arm from the elbow, squeezed back on the trigger and shot the youngster through the chest. Mann was driven back against the end of the seat hard, head coming forward, a gout of bright blood spewing from his mouth on to the floor.

Hardin cursed and pulled his pistol free from under his coat just as the Ranger captain lashed out with his cane. It struck the gunman on the side of the wrist and knocked arm and weapon aside, a .44 slug discharging through the window and shattering it outwards.

Close by Hardin, Mason threw his hands above his head and shouted that he had no gun.

Armstrong jumped Hardin, grabbing for his gun hand, missing the hand itself but seizing the barrel of his pistol. Armstrong brought round his own pistol fast and smacked the side of the long barrel alongside Hardin's temple. The gunfighter's legs shook but refused to give way. Both men struggled for control of Hardin's .44, Ollie Halverton looking for a chance to intervene.

Outside, Wes Hart heard a shout at his back and saw the door to the adjoining coach swing open. The man who came running through had a six-gun in one hand, a whisky bottle in the other.

'Hold it there!' called Hart.

Daley Carson kept on coming.

Hart shot him through the fleshy part of the right shoulder and Carson lurched back against the door and dropped the bottle crashing down the steps.

'Christ!' he yelled and went tumbling after it.

Hart waited until he'd finished rolling and clubbed him unconscious with the butt end of his Colt.

O'Reilly was running along the platform. A lot of folk were shouting and screaming. Back inside the coach Jimmy Mann had got to his feet and evaded Ollie, jumping on to one of the seats. Ollie called for him to stay where he was. Mann threw himself through the already shattered window and on to the boards of the platform.

Armstrong brought the barrel of his gun down on Hardin's temple for the third time. There was blood over both of them, most of it Hardin's.

Out on the platform, Jimmy Mann somehow got to his knees, blood thick on his shirt. O'Reilly took careful aim and kicked into the centre of his face, breaking his nose in two places.

Masters was down on all fours against one of the seats, Lamar leaning over him, the tip of his pistol barrel resting on the nape of Masters' neck. Apart from a lot of unsteady breathing, neither man was moving.

Wes Hart came into the coach as Armstrong was hauling

Hardin to his feet, a lot of pride showing through the splashings of blood.

'Let's get this trash outside!' he said.

Climbing down the steps to the platform, his wrists manacled together and Armstrong's pistol square at the small of his back, Hardin caught sight of Wes Hart.

'You bastard!' he yelled. 'I said I'd kill you . . .'

He raised his hands high and jumped off the steps towards Hart, intending to pummel him to the ground. As he was in mid-air, Armstrong thrust his cane high between his legs, tripping him. Hart neatly side-stepped and drew his holstered Colt. The fast arc of it struck Hardin's forehead hard enough to break the skin and draw a gouging line of blood.

'You said it okay.' Hart stood over him. 'You said it an', you mean an' miserable bastard, you was wrong!'

On 1 October 1878, John Wesley Hardin was sentenced to twenty-five years in the Texas State Penitentiary for the murder of Deputy Sheriff Charles Webb. In prison he studied law between periods of hard labour and was released and pardoned on 17th February 1894. His wife, Jane, died while he was in the penitentiary.

Released, he set up a law office in Gonzales, Texas, then moved to Junction. Here he met and married a young girl called Callie Lewis, who left him on the same day as their wedding. Hardin moved to El Paso, still attempting to practise law. He took up with a crew of gamblers and low-lifes and crossed two El Paso policemen, the Selmans, father and son. After some public arguing the older Selman, a former Texan gunfighter, walked up behind Hardin while he was shooting dice and shot him through the back of the head. The bullet tore his skull and emerged through his eye.

Wes Hart quit the Texas Rangers on the last day of August, 1877. He rode into New Mexico and fought for John Chisum in the Lincoln County Range War. Along with Dick Brewer and a skinny youngster named Billy Bonney, he was one of Chisum's and Tunstall's unofficial posse of Regulators. When Hart left New Mexico and struck out for Indian Territory on his own, the name Regulator just stuck.